"I know you've take___ ___ false identity, that y___ ___ mild-mannered professor."

Heather knew? Alex's mind was racing. All that work to establish his cover, and in a flash it was blown?

"Who are you working for, Alex?"

He had to remain calm. But the sight of Heather in her pajamas was almost more than he could bear. He was strong, he was tough. He was the agency's top secret agent. He wasn't going to let one small little wisp of a woman do him in.

"I have no idea what you're talking about."

"It's okay." She took his hand in hers and he felt a searing heat wash over him. "You probably got into it accidentally."

Alex shook his head. "You need to sit down. You're obviously not thinking clearly." He led her over to the kitchen table. Then out of the corner of his eye he caught a glimpse of his gun, peeking out of the shoulder holster slung over the chair.

He had to distract her! But how?

One sure way came to mind....

Dear Reader,

As you head for your favorite vacation hideaway, don't forget to bring along some Special Edition novels for sensational summertime reading!

This month's THAT'S MY BABY! title commemorates Diana Whitney's twenty-fifth Silhouette novel! *I Now Pronounce You Mom & Dad,* which also launches her FOR THE CHILDREN miniseries, is a poignant story about two former flames who conveniently wed for the sake of their beloved godchildren. Look for book two, *A Dad of His Own,* in September in the Silhouette Romance line, and book three, *The Fatherhood Factor,* in Special Edition in October.

Bestselling author Joan Elliott Pickart wraps up her captivating THE BACHELOR BET series with a heart-stirring love story between an amnesiac beauty and a brooding doctor in *The Most Eligible M.D.* The excitement continues with *Beth and the Bachelor* by reader favorite Susan Mallery—a romantic tale about a suburban mom who is swept off her feet by her very own Prince Charming. And fall in love with a virile *Secret Agent Groom,* book two in Andrea Edwards's THE BRIDAL CIRCLE series, about a shy Plain Jane who is powerfully drawn to her mesmerizing new neighbor.

Rounding out this month, Jennifer Mikels delivers an emotional reunion romance that features a rodeo champ who returns to his hometown to make up for lost time with the woman he loves... and the son he never knew existed, in *Forever Mine.* And family secrets are unveiled when a sophisticated lady melts a gruff cowboy's heart in *A Family Secret* by Jean Brashear.

I hope you enjoy each of these romances—where dreams come true!

Best,

Karen Taylor Richman
Senior Editor

Please address questions and book requests to:
Silhouette Reader Service
U.S.: 3010 Walden Ave., P.O. Box 1325, Buffalo, NY 14269
Canadian: P.O. Box 609, Fort Erie, Ont. L2A 5X3

ANDREA EDWARDS

SECRET AGENT GROOM

Silhouette®

SPECIAL EDITION®

Published by Silhouette Books

America's Publisher of Contemporary Romance

To all the "Heathers" the world over who take in the stray, abandoned and feral cats and dogs, and give them food and shelter and most of all love.
Jamie, Tam, Sima, Marilyn, Judy, Paula, Linda and Scott, Lorrie, Margery, Denise, Debby, DeAnna, Marlise and all the countless others who never turn and look the other way—this one's for you.

 SILHOUETTE BOOKS

ISBN 0-373-24264-6

SECRET AGENT GROOM

Visit us at www.romance.net

Printed in U.S.A.

ANDREA EDWARDS

is the pseudonym of Anne and Ed Kolaczyk, a husband-and-wife writing team who have been telling their stories for more than fifteen years. Anne is a former elementary school teacher, while Ed is a refugee from corporate America. After many years in the Chicago area, they now live in a small town in northern Indiana where they are avid students of local history, family legends and ethnic myths. Recently they have both been bitten by the gardening bug, but only time will tell how serious the affliction is. Their four children are grown, but remaining at home with Anne and Ed are two dogs, four cats and one bird—not the same ones that first walked through their stories but carrying on the same tradition of chaotic rule of the household nonetheless.

To: Mrs. Angela Smith
Memorial Hospital Thrift Shop
Chesterton, Indiana

Dear Mrs. Smith,

Thank you so much for sending that envelope
of personal items back to me. I had no idea
it was in that carton of old clothes I cleaned
out of the attic and donated to the thrift shop.

I'm afraid, however, that your congratulations
are unnecessary. The papers in the envelope
aren't plans for my approaching wedding, but
from a silly club called The Bridal Circle my
best girlfriends and I formed way back in high
school. We'd planned what we thought would be
the perfect weddings, and as you saw, mine was
an elopement. No fuss, no agonizing over guest
lists and dresses and menus—just pure
romance. Silly, wasn't it?

And I have no idea how Alex Waterstone's name
got on that personality quiz. I'm sure I didn't
put it there. We didn't move in the same circles
back then any more than we do now. I suspect
one of my friends was playing a joke on me.

Thanks again for returning the envelope—and
the sweet memories. I got a good laugh at
remembering how silly I was back then.

Yours truly,

Heather Mahoney

Heather Mahoney

Prologue

"Let's tell ghost stories," Dorothy suggested, pushing aside her scrapbook and stretching out on her sleeping bag, her best childhood girlfriends scattered around her.

Ghost stories? Heather's breath abandoned her and her mouth went dry.

"Oo, that'll be fun." Penny sat up quickly, like the idea was exciting, the newspaper and magazine cuttings of the royal wedding apparently forgotten around her.

Heather just gulped back her panic. She turned around and stared out the screen door into the darkness of Penny's family's tree farm, then returned her gaze to the safety of the family room. It was Penny's slumber party, Heather told herself, and her friend had a right to do what she wanted, but even so.

Karin was on her feet. "We can turn out the lights and I'll—"

The lights out? "No!"

The three girls all turned to stare at Heather. She tried to say something but her mouth was too dry. She tried to even think of something to say, but her brain didn't seem to be working. Finally, after a deep breath, she forced a smile.

"We haven't finished our scrapbooks," she said.

"Oh, who cares?" Karin asked and reached for the light. "This'll be much more fun."

Fun? Being so scared you couldn't sleep was fun?

By the age of eight, Heather Anne Mahoney knew some things were absolutely, positively true. If she played in the woods near Lake Palomara, she'd get bitten by rabid raccoons and bats and weasels, and would swell up and die a horrible death like that little girl Great-Aunt Millie's cousin knew. If she left her window open at night in the summer, she'd catch a chill and get pneumonia and die from a terrible high fever like the little boy that used to live next door to old Mrs. Schubert's mother's best friend. And if she went outside in a storm, she would get struck by lightning and be fried to death with her hair all smoking like the man somebody who used to work with Grandpa Mahoney at the sawmill knew.

By the time she was twelve, Heather had added a few more truths to her list. Boys were always up to no good—though no one would tell her just what that meant. Nobody liked a smart aleck, or a braggart, or a Goody Two-shoes, or a party pooper. And if she made a mistake in public, no one would ever let her forget it.

And now that she was fourteen, she was well versed

in all the dangers the world held—most of which the rest of the world didn't recognize.

"You're not scared, are you?" Karin asked.

"Why would she be scared?" Dorothy laughed at the idea. "They're just stories. Heather knows that."

But Penny gave her a long, knowing look. "What would you rather do instead?" she asked gently.

Heather felt a double whammy of guilt fall onto her shoulders. Penny was so nice. Heather should agree to the ghost stories; it was what Penny wanted to do, after all. But what if there really were such things as ghosts and talking about them made them wake up and then they came—

Heather's eyes locked onto the picture of the princess in her wedding dress and she grabbed ahold of the idea. "Let's plan our weddings," she suggested.

"Plan our weddings?" Karin's voice held nothing but boredom and disdain, making Heather wince. "What in the world for?"

"For fun," Heather said. "We'll plan our weddings and write it all out so we'll remember it ten years from now."

"If we don't need the plans for ten years, we can wait a few days to make them," Karin said, still standing by the light. "And tell ghost stories tonight."

"We can still do both," Dorothy pointed out. She closed her scrapbook and sat cross-legged on the sofa. "So where do we start?"

With a loud sigh, Karin plopped down on the sofa next to Penny. Heather tried not to look at the annoyance dancing clearly across Karin's face. It would be all right. Karin would see how much fun this was once they got started.

"You probably just all want a wedding like Princess

Diana's," Karin said. "Big ruffly dress. Rich important husband. And a horse-drawn carriage decorated with flowers. There, we're done."

Heather took a deep breath and hugged her pillow to her. "I don't want a wedding like that," she said.

"You don't?" Dorothy sounded surprised. "I think it would be perfect."

"With all those people watching you?" Heather asked.

"Well, maybe not half the world," Dorothy admitted. She took a handful of popcorn and looked away with a dreamy smile on her face. "But I would love a dress like that with a long train and flowers everywhere."

"I want to get married outside," Penny said. "In a garden filled with flowers."

"Your train would get all dirty," Karin noted.

"I wouldn't have one. Just a simple dress and a short veil." Penny picked up her soda and sipped at it. "Maybe flowers in my hair instead of a veil."

"You know what I think would be the most romantic thing ever?" Heather said. "To elope."

Her three friends stared at her, surprise hovering in the air. Dorothy stopped munching on popcorn. Penny stopped drinking her soda and Karin stopped frowning.

"Elope?" Karin finally repeated.

Heather nodded. "To be so much in love that you don't want anything but each other. Wouldn't that be the most wonderful thing?"

"But wouldn't you want your family and friends at your wedding?" Penny asked.

"Maybe we'd have a party later and invite everyone."

Karin shook her head. "What about throwing the rice and tying tin cans to your car?"

"Rice is bad for the birds."

Dorothy sat up. "But if you eloped all of Chesterton wouldn't be at your wedding."

"Right, so Alex Waterstone won't be racing across the seawall." Heather shuddered at the thought of the town daredevil. "He's the very last person I'd want at my wedding."

Chapter One

"Is it raining there?" Edith Mahoney's worry came over the telephone lines loud and clear. "I saw on the TV that it was raining in northern Indiana. You've got your windows closed, don't you?"

Heather leaned over the kitchen counter to look up at the evening sky. "It's not raining, Mom. It's not even cloudy here."

"The weather channel doesn't lie," her mother said. "Maybe you should go in the basement, just in case. The middle of August is still tornado season."

Heather straightened up. Her dinner was waiting on the kitchen table but she hated to eat while she talked. Not that she really believed that old wives' tale about choking on your food, but there was no reason to take chances.

"Mom, I'm fine. Maybe the storm is east of us."

"At least turn on your TV, so you'll see the storm

warnings," her mother said, then sighed loudly. "Your father and I should never have moved out here. If we were there now, his knee would tell us if a storm was coming."

Heather wanted to hug her mother for her concern, but wished she could actually make her stop worrying. Heather was thirty-three years old, for goodness sake, not thirteen. But this was a battle Heather was never going to win.

"It's just that you need a man around." Her mother launched into her favorite refrain. "What'll you do if a tree falls on your house?"

"I'll call Penny's tree service."

But her mother went on as if Heather hadn't spoken. "What if you find a mouse in your house?"

"The cats will take care of it."

"What if you hear a noise in the middle of the night?"

Heather always heard noises in the middle of the night, and found burrowing deep under the covers was just as effective as getting up to investigate. And if that didn't work, her bed was high enough to hide under. Or there was the closet.

But that wasn't what her mother needed to hear. "If someone's breaking in, I'll call the police," she assured her.

"Heather!" her mother wailed. "I'm serious. You're all alone in Chesterton and I worry about you."

But Heather wasn't all alone. She had lots of friends who would help her if she needed help. "Mom, if something happens and I need help right away, I could always call Alex."

"Alex Waterstone?" Heather could feel her mother's shiver of horror. "I'd rather Godzilla lived next door to you."

"Mom, Alex is fine. Well, I don't know him very well but he seems nice enough."

"Nice?" Her mother's voice was practically a shriek. "I'll never forget the nightmares you had after he raced across the seawall on his bike."

"He doesn't race across seawalls anymore, Mom. He's a college professor, very dull and proper." Though to be honest, he didn't look all that dull and proper. She was sure his female students fell madly in love with him. "But I imagine he could catch a mouse for me if he had to."

"I doubt it," her mother was going on. "I saw him when I was in town last and he's turned into the biggest namby-pamby I ever saw."

Heather had to laugh. In spite of his hunky looks, wild child Alex had turned into a very sedate adult. "Well, either way, you don't have to worry. Alex Waterstone and I hardly ever talk. I doubt that he's taken his nose out of his poetry books long enough to notice my existence."

"Hmph." Her mother snorted. "Well, his loss."

Heather bit back another laugh as she turned, sensing movement in the backyard. Sure enough, a small gray animal was darting across the flower bed, then disappeared into the rose bushes. That feral kitten was back.

"Mom, can I go? That kitten I've been trying to catch is back."

"I just wish you would go after men the way you go after cats," her mother said with a sigh. "Well, be careful, dear. Wear gloves."

* * *

Alex Waterstone pulled into the restaurant parking lot and got out of his car—a book of poetry in his hand and his regulation SIG-Sauer .380 automatic in his ankle holster. Relaxed and in control, he strolled into the diner. Life was good. After spending interminable months setting up his cover, the damn investigation was finally getting in gear.

Two fellow agents were sitting in a booth in the back. Dressed casually in short-sleeved cotton shirts and slacks, their nondescriptness made them blend in perfectly. Alex slid into the booth to join them. No one in the diner paid any attention to them.

"Any problems?" Fitzgerald asked under his breath.

"You weren't spotted, were you?" Casio, Alex's supervisor, asked.

The vinyl bench felt sticky and Alex had sudden visions of being forever cemented in place. Permanence, the ultimate horror. A lifetime ticking away a micromillisecond at a time. But he just grinned. "Problems? Why would a respected professor of literature at Midwest University have any problems?"

Casio groaned. "Don't start. We can't afford to be here all night."

"The only problem I have is what rhyme scheme to use for my next poem." Alex left his poetry book on the table for effect, then glanced at the menu left at his place. He really wasn't hungry at all, still riding high on adrenaline, but when the waitress came over, he ordered something anyway. "Iced tea and the salad bar."

The waitress took his menu and went into the kitchen, leaving the three men isolated in the back corner of the restaurant.

"So what's the word?" Alex asked.

Casio pushed his half-eaten salad aside. "It's a go for tomorrow."

"Hot damn." It seemed like they'd been waiting forever.

He'd needed to play it safe to build his cover, but it had been too safe for too long. If things hadn't started soon, he would have been back to racing across the seawall in a storm for excitement. But would it have been the same thrill at thirty-four that it had been at fourteen? He pulled over the folder of photos Casio had brought. "Now, who's who here?"

For the next hour, while they ate, they pored over pictures and background sketches of all the known thugs in this operation, what they knew of the gambling setup, how they could best infiltrate it. And how they could minimize the risks. These guys were known to shoot first and ask questions later.

"I'm ready to go tonight," Alex said. "Why are we waiting until tomorrow?"

"Writing poetry isn't exciting enough for you?" Casio asked.

"My granny always said to be careful what you wish for," Fitz said. "There is such a thing as too much excitement."

Alex took a deep breath. They didn't understand. "I'm craving to get these guys behind bars. That's all."

Casio laughed. "Yeah, right. You just want to retire to Chesterton and spend your days writing poems about *The Wizard of Oz*."

"Hey, maybe he's got an eye on some coed," Fitz said with a snicker. "Or maybe he wants to put down roots with some single neighbor lady who bakes him cookies."

Alex's stomach tightened up. Even after working together for five years, they sure didn't know him. Retirement was for those who'd lost their nerve. Roots were for those who wanted to be hurt.

But he just smiled at his fellow agents. "Mrs. Fallon lives to the south of me. She's a sixty-five-year-old widow who never gives me anything but her dead husband's advice. A younger single woman lives to the north but she hasn't talked to me since grade school. She doesn't bake me cookies, either."

"Maybe she's got the hots for you but is shy."

Alex pulled over the stack of photos they'd been studying. "Maybe you need a life."

He forced them back to their casework, annoyed with himself and with his partners. They should know him better and he shouldn't overreact to their stupid jokes. It was all proof that he needed a jolt of action. Everything was getting to him lately, including—or maybe mostly—living in Chesterton.

The agency'd thought going back to his hometown would be the perfect cover, but they hadn't thought through all he'd have to do to blend in. Everything from renewing old friendships to serving on committees for the Wizard of Oz festival held each September. Even Heather Mahoney and her silence was getting to him. She had been standing right next to him for a good part of the poetry reading last week and had barely said a word. Action on this case had come at the right moment.

"We all set then?" Casio asked.

"Two o'clock tomorrow." Alex carefully folded up the scrap of paper with the address and put it in his pants pocket. "I'll be there."

It was dark by the time they parted, each leaving

separately and going in different directions. Alex kept to a careful speed, just below the limit, but his heart was racing with excitement.

Phase one of the operation was going smoothly. He was set in his role as a professor at Midwest University, newly appointed to handle the tutoring program for the athletic department. His student tutors had already started helping the football players keep up with their schoolwork.

Now phase two was set to start tomorrow. If things went right, he'd gain entrance into the private gambling club and prove himself to be a heavy better. In a week, he'd be deeply mired in gambling debt, borrowing heavily and losing more. In two weeks, just about the time Midwest's first football game would be played, he should be approached to put a few key players on academic probation. In a month, he'd be expected to guarantee certain games would be a loss. In two months, indictments would go down and some of the world's worst scum would have their gambling operation shut down, cutting off a major source of funds for their other corrupt activities.

Alex grinned. This was better than the seawall at its stormiest. It was the life he was born to. He wished he had discovered it sooner, before he'd spent four years in grad school on a degree his mother wanted more than he did. But she'd seemed so desperate to believe that Alex had outgrown his wild streak, that he'd done what he could to make her happy.

But had it been a wild streak he could outgrow, or part of who he was?

Alex turned onto his street, glad to be nearing home. He should go jogging tonight and spend an hour or so lifting weights. He wanted to be ready for tomorrow.

Even as he planned out the rest of his evening, he peered through the darkness, automatically checking out his house in the block up ahead. He hit the scanner button on the security monitor clipped to his car visor. Not that anyone had ever—

The monitor buzzed. Alex was stunned for a second, then glanced at the small LED panel. The perimeter system had been breached, not the house system. Someone had gone into the yard. He hit another button. The system had been breached only once, at 9:55 p.m. So whoever had come into the yard was still there after ten minutes. It probably wasn't a kid getting a ball that had accidentally gone into the yard.

His heart racing, he turned at a side street and pulled into the alley a block south of his house. His movements quick and sure, he slipped out of the car, silently closing the door, then stepped into the cover of some overgrown bushes as he pulled out his gun. Damn. This couldn't be a coincidence. Not the night before the operation began. Could he have been followed? Or had he been made earlier?

He crept down the alley toward his house, his feet crunching ever so slightly on the sparse gravel. Music came from one house, the sounds of a TV from another, dancing lightly in the moist evening air. He moved from the bushes to the deep shadow of a garage to the high stockade fence behind Mrs. Fallon's house. The lighting in the alley was spotty and it wasn't hard to stay hidden.

Unless someone was watching for him, of course.

Just past Mrs. Fallon's yard, he squatted down to watch his house, looking for the slightest movement. His yard was enclosed with wire fencing and he could see his house from his distant vantage point. A high pole light with an automatic switch lit up the yard at night. But he saw nothing. Could the alarm have malfunctioned? Accidentally set off? Possible but not likely.

So what had happened? Had his cover been blown? And, if it had, by whom? An icy calm seeped through his veins. It didn't matter who, not right now. What mattered was that he wasn't some wet-behind-the-ears rookie who would get caught unawares. He knew what he was doing.

He heard a sound, sensed a movement coming from behind his detached garage, and smiled slowly. He couldn't have asked for a better spot. With the garage on one side and the fence and bushes on two others, there was only one way out of that small corner. And that's where he would be.

Using a low branch from a tree, he vaulted quietly over the fence and into his yard. The movement continued without pause. He hadn't been noticed. Closer and closer he crept. It was almost too easy.

That thought made him halt and pull back into the shadows. But there were no signs of anyone else, and he'd have his back to the garage so he wouldn't be vulnerable. Two final steps and he swung out into the open, his gun drawn and pointed at the figure behind the lilac bush.

"Freeze," he cried.

In the lights from the alley, he saw blond hair pulled into a braid and then blue eyes flashed up at him. Wide startled eyes that reminded him of a deer caught in the headlights of a car.

His body turned to ice for a moment, then anger, fury, rage raced over him. He lowered his gun.

"Heather?" he bellowed. What the hell was she doing here? He could have shot her. Didn't she have any sense? But he took a deep deep breath, cleared his throat and tried to find a professorial voice. "What an unforeseen delight! Might I be of assistance to you?"

Heather just stared at Alex. And at the gun in his hand. Her heart had stopped and in a moment she would be dead. If she was lucky, that is. Otherwise, Alex would certainly—

She gulped and blinked and when she looked again, he was tying his shoes and there was no gun. Of course, there wasn't. He was an English professor, for goodness sake. A poet. He wouldn't have a gun. She had imagined it. Her stomach always tightened up around him and now her brain was, too, dreaming up things that weren't there.

She gulped and blinked again, since it had worked the first time, but she was still in her pajamas sitting on the damp ground in Alex's backyard and he was still frowning at her.

"Heather?" he said as he stood back up. "Did you mislay something?"

She realized suddenly he wasn't just frowning at her, he'd been talking to her. Action was required, or at least some response. Great, now what? She tried to stand up, but her knees didn't seem to want to support her. If she'd been one of her kindergarten kids, she would've cried, or blamed one of the other kids, or talked about something else.

"Great poetry reading last week," she said brightly but it came out dimly. More like dumbly. That was the all-time stupidest remark that had ever come out of her mouth.

"Yes, it was quite edifying," Alex replied. His

voice was cautious, as if he wasn't sure if she was dangerous or not. "Might I inquire the reasons why you are reposing out here in…"

"My pajamas?" she finished for him. They looked like a T-shirt and shorts, but she knew the snoozing kitties all over them gave it away.

"Uh…" He paused, almost as if he was at a loss for words. "I had thought to say 'out here in the darkness.'"

"Oh." He hadn't known, not until she'd told him. She closed her eyes briefly and sank up to her chin in mortification. Where were the poisonous spiders when you needed them?

Opening her eyes, she looked back up at Alex. He was the handsomest male in all of Indiana—dark hair falling slightly over his forehead, tall and broadshouldered—and he scared the wits out of her. Somehow, since he moved back to Chesterton last year and accepted the professorship at MU, he seemed even more dangerous than he had as a kid, which was crazy.

"I saw a kitten run into your yard," she admitted. "I tried to catch her earlier this evening and couldn't. I didn't think you'd mind if I followed her to try again."

"A kitten?" He sounded only slightly exasperated and squatted down next to her to peer under the bushes.

"She's back in there." Heather got onto her hands and knees and picked up her flashlight, holding it so that the light filtered gently through the leaves and just barely showed the tiny creature in the mouth of the pipe. "There's some kind of drainage pipe that she's sitting in."

Alex moved closer to her. Too close, actually. As he leaned forward to look under the bush he brushed against her arm—just her arm, for heaven's sake! But her whole body blushed a bright red, while her temperature soared.

Good heavens! She couldn't react this way to Alex. He was the last man on earth she could be attracted to.

"The kitten's quite small," he said.

Heather moved over a few inches—to a spot that she could see better from—and looked in also. The little gray kitten was barely visible in the deep shadows, but Heather could feel her fear.

"The poor baby," she said. "She must be—"

Alex reached in and grabbed at the animal. There was a hiss and a tiny snarl—then Alex drew back quickly.

"Hey!" he said as he sat back on his heels. "She bit me." He shook his hand as if it stung.

"Oh, it's my fault," Heather cried. "I should have told you right away she was feral. You didn't realize it since I wasn't using a trap. I'm so sorry. I shouldn't have let you reach in there like that."

She took Alex's hand and looked at the narrow streak of blood on his palm, feeling a rush of relief. Or was it a rush of something else? Her cheeks felt as if they were aflame suddenly and she quickly let go.

"It's just a scratch, not a bite," she said. "We'll wash it up but I don't think it's anything to worry about."

"I wasn't worried," Alex informed her. "And you didn't exactly 'let' me reach in, you know. I did it myself."

His voice sounded brusque, but she didn't blame him. He probably was tired, and annoyed to find her here.

"Are you sure the kitten did it?" she asked.

"Maybe it was a stinging nettle. They can be poisonous sometimes, you know, and once I think I found one in my yard."

He was staring at her again with that same look of exasperation. Or maybe pity. "It was the kitten," he said. "Honest. She was telling me to bug off."

Bug off? This was staid, dignified Professor Waterstone? No, it sounded more like Alex "Just Watch Me!" Waterstone. The boy who jumped from the Sheridans' oak tree to the Cauldwells' garage while she was screaming at him not to. The teen who liked to go snake hunting around Lake Palomara and bring boxes of his catches to show around the neighborhood. The high school senior who spray-painted Go Chesterton on arch rival Valparaiso's water tower.

She wished he would go inside his house or would remember he needed something at the store. He was making her nervous just by sitting here next to her. She took a deep breath and turned to peer back under the bush.

"I hope you told her we weren't going to bug off." Heather set the flashlight in the bush, facing away from the pipe so that only a soft light was thrown around the kitten. "And that a certain little kitten is going to be sleeping inside tonight."

"Oh, yeah," Alex said. "All that and more."

Heather just concentrated on opening the little can of tuna from her rescue kit and tried not to think about Alex watching her. Or about the fact that these pajamas were not made of very thick material. Or that catching a feral kitten was more interesting than Heather could ever be.

She dumped the tuna onto a small plate. *Do what*

you came to do, she ordered herself. *Then get back home where you belong.*

She pushed the plate slowly toward the drainage pipe. "There you go, sweetums," she said softly. "Doesn't that smell yummy? I bet you're hungry, aren't you?"

A soft little cry came in response and the kitten poked her small head out of the pipe.

"That's the idea," Alex said. "Come on out and chow down."

Heather started slightly. Alex was laying on the ground next to her, peering under the bush also. He was going to help her?

No matter how she tried not to care, the idea made her warm, both inside and out. She turned her own attention quickly back to the kitten. At least she knew what she was doing there. Trying to understand Alex— or any man—was way beyond her.

"You want some yummy tuna?" she coaxed and cooed to the kitten. "Come on, sugar pie. You don't have to be afraid. I won't let mean old Uncle Alex get you."

"Mean old Uncle Alex?" he repeated under his breath.

Heather didn't reply because the kitten was inching out of the pipe, drawn by the smell of the fish, and she needed to focus on that. Thank goodness, for she didn't know what had possessed her to say that out loud. She never did things like that. Maybe she had been pricked by the poisonous nettle and was acting irrationally. She needed to get this kitten and get back home.

"Come on, little honey," she murmured and shifted her weight slightly. "You just come over and eat."

The kitten was almost all the way out of the pipe.

Another step and she was out. Another step and she was almost to the plate. One more and she was sniffing the tuna cautiously. Then—

Heather swooped in, grabbed the kitten by the scruff of the neck and, despite her loud protests, put her into a terry-cloth bag. Once Heather'd closed off the neck of the bag with her hand, the kitten went silent. Heather got to her feet.

"That's it?" Alex said, standing also. "Want me to carry that?"

Heather tightened her hold on the bag as she bent down. "No, thanks. I've got it." Just how was she supposed to escape her weird reactions to Alex if she didn't get away from him? "I'll just get the rest—"

But he got her flashlight before she could. And the plate of tuna. "Should I just dump this?"

She closed her eyes briefly. She should take it from him. She should tell him to throw it away. She should remember how she'd been afraid to sit near him on the school bus, for fear he would have bugs to show her or would hang half out the window to pick an apple from a tree they were passing. But all she could think of was that she couldn't carry everything.

She opened her eyes, smiled at Alex and stepped off the cliff. "This little girl earned her tuna. Can you bring it over to my place?"

"Sure."

So she led him over to her house—barefoot, in her pajamas and with the certainty in her stomach that she was an idiot. He seemed nice and polite and trustworthy, but he was still Alex Waterstone. She was still afraid of him. Things happened around him. Why couldn't that nice shoe salesman that just moved in two blocks down have come to help her? She pulled open her back screen door and went into the kitchen. Alex followed her.

"You can leave the other stuff on the kitchen table," she said and took another deep breath. "Want to bring the plate of tuna down here?"

He put the plate and flashlight down. "Down where?" he asked.

This was probably a gigantic mistake. He obviously didn't want to be here and she should be getting her silly heart in line. She could hardly do that with him by her side. Still, she turned toward the hall. "Come on down to the strays' room."

"The strays' room?"

She'd turned and was heading down the back hallway. He was right behind her, making her wish she'd stopped to put a coat on. Except that would have looked really dumb. He was coming to see the kitten, not her.

"I do rescue work for Pet Refuge," she told him over her shoulder. "I foster some of their cats until they get a home of their own. When they first come, they go into quarantine here in the strays' room."

"Oh."

She went into the small bedroom, flicking on the light. A large empty dog crate was in the corner, a blanket draped over the top and three sides. She opened the crate's door, leaned inside and put the terrycloth bag in the back, leaving it open slightly. Then she slipped her hand out of the crate and secured its door.

"What's with the cage?" Alex asked, his voice suddenly suspicious and annoyed.

Heather sighed. She'd been through this before.

"The kitten's feral," she said. "She needs to be force-socialized."

"Force-socialized?" He'd gone from sounding annoyed to sounding outraged. "What are you going to do? Refuse to feed her unless she's friendly?"

"No," Heather said as she took the plate of tuna from him. "But I do have to touch her and hold her every few hours, whether she wants me to or not."

"That'll just scare her more."

"At first, yes," Heather agreed, quickly opening the crate door and slipping the plate of food into the cage. The kitten poked its nose out from under the towel, sniffing the air. Once they left, she'd be out for her reward.

"But it's for her own good," Heather continued. "She'll never find a home if she's afraid of people."

"Oh. I hadn't thought of that." His anger had disappeared. "Guess it would be hard to find a home for a cat who hissed and scratched whoever came near."

His tone had almost started to disarm her, but his words brought her back to earth with a jolt. His scratch!

"We need to wash that scratch of yours," she said. "I don't know what I was thinking of."

"I'm fine," he said.

"It needs to be cleaned," she insisted and went past him back into the hall. "Come on. I have some disinfectant wash."

"It's not a big deal," he said and glanced at his hand. "I can't even see where it was."

"It'll be a big deal if your hand gets infected and falls off," she said.

"It's not going to fall off."

They were in the kitchen by that time, and the spacious room felt small suddenly. Small and awfully well lit. A calico cat was on the table, busily licking out the empty tuna can, and Heather jumped at the distraction.

"Victoria," Heather scolded and put the cat onto the floor. "Would you behave, please?"

Victoria just sat under the table, looking offended, but not providing Heather with any more distraction. She hurried over to her first-aid supplies, and pulled a bottle from the cabinet.

"Here, wash your hands with this."

He took the bottle from her and turned to the sink.

She relaxed slightly and watched his hands as he washed. She'd never noticed what nice hands he had. Large, but strong. Protective. Like they'd—

She frowned as a puckered whitish scar on the back of his right hand came into view. "How'd you do that?" she asked.

Alex looked at it, then over at her and shrugged. "I don't know," he said. "Must have gotten it as a kid, fooling around."

How could you not remember getting a scar like that? And he never got hurt as a kid, that was what was so scary. You just knew with his next stunt something terrible would happen, but it never did. She spotted another scar, this one a long red streak on his upper arm.

"How'd you do that?" she asked.

But he just laughed and shook his hands dry over the sink before picking up the towel she'd left for him. "I'm afraid I don't remember that one, either. Maybe from that time I fell off the Cauldwells' garage," he said.

He was lying. He hadn't fallen off. But maybe he'd

gotten the scars in some embarrassing way. Or maybe he just thought it was none of her business.

Or maybe she was right. Things did happen around him. Scary things.

He put the towel down. "Well, I guess I'll be getting on home."

"Thank you for your help. You've really been nice about all this."

"How should I have been?" he asked.

"Oh, I don't know. You seemed stuffier since you came back to town. Somehow I even thought you talked stuffier."

"Talked stuffier?" His voice sounded odd. Sort of strangled. "Perhaps catching feral felines is a less formal endeavor."

He seemed to change, seemed to become someone else right before her eyes and it sent a chill all the way down her spine and into her toes. What was going on?

"Yes, that must be it," she said slowly, her stomach tightening into a little ball of nerves. "Thanks again for your help."

"My pleasure entirely." He nodded and pulled his keys from his pants pocket as he turned to the door.

Heather watched him leave, listened as the sound of the screen door closing echoed in the dark stillness. She heard his footsteps on the sidewalk, then the sound of his door. Then the night was hers again.

"Well, Victoria, I think we can breathe now," she said. "We got safely through our encounter with Professor Alex Waterstone."

But Victoria had been joined by Heather's other cat, Henry, and they were both playing with something on the floor. Heather hurried over, hoping it wasn't a bug.

It wasn't. It was a piece of paper with an address on it. Alex must have dropped it.

Chapter Two

Alex let himself into his house, reset the security system, grabbed a soda then sat down in his dark living room and stared out at the quiet little street that ran in front of his house. The old-fashioned streetlights barely competed with the moonlight, and the soft sounds of summer tiptoed in through his open windows.

A typical summer's night in Chesterton. One that normally would have soothed him, quieted whatever nerves had been jangled that day, but it wasn't working tonight.

He found himself tense and on edge. And not on his good adrenaline high anymore, either. His feelings were now of the irritable variety. He was dissatisfied about some nameless thing but felt helpless to do anything about it and he didn't like that. Not one damn little bit.

He took a quick pull on his soda can and tried to bring himself around.

Hell, that situation with Heather was actually funny. And the way he'd finessed things with his gun was good. He'd been lucky that it had been dark. Otherwise, even a civilian like Heather would have spotted the weapon he'd been pointing at her.

Anyway. All's well that ends well. Although…

A picture of petite Heather, barefoot, and in her pajamas filled his mind, pushing out the moonlight-dappled scene outside. There was something about her smile that tugged at him, something about the wistfulness that filled her eyes. He almost felt guilty for having misled her—which was crazy. She was the one who'd come into his yard and had set off the security alarm. Although that wasn't her fault, either.

He should have been laughing about tonight's incident but he found himself growing moodier.

Heather had always been so sensitive. If you looked at her the wrong way, she'd be off crying. Not that she'd done any of that tonight. No, she was competent and determined. She was going to rescue that kitten and she knew exactly how to go about it.

Suddenly he noticed where his mind was going and he frowned. Whoa. What was the matter with him? Still in his thirties and he was growing all nostalgic like an old man sitting on his front porch, beer in hand, watching the fireflies dance in the night.

Suddenly flashing red-and-blue lights outside called for his attention and Alex gratefully gave it. It looked like a police car, running with lights but no sirens. Was there a burglary in progress? He got up and walked to his window, where his mouth dropped open. It was pulling up in front of his house.

Oh, hell. It had to be the agency. They'd been monitoring his security system and had called the local gendarmes. Damn.

Alex turned some lights on, put down his soda can, and went to the door to greet the officer coming up his walk, sidearm drawn.

"Evening, Toto." Alex stepped out onto his front porch. "To what do I owe the pleasure?"

"Hi, Alex," the policeman said with a smile. "How are you?"

"Splendid. Could not possibly be better." Alex paused, then pretended confusion. "What occasion sends you to my home?"

Toto shrugged. "Got a call that something was wrong here."

"At my home?" Alex frowned. "What is thought to be amiss?"

Toto shook his head. "Don't rightly know. I was just supposed to check things out."

Alex quickly stepped aside. "Well, by all means. Please do. I would not feel safe until you ascertain things are secure."

The policeman sighed, then went inside the house. Alex just waited on the porch, leaning against the porch railing, watching the lights in Heather's house next door. He saw a calico cat in the window of a darkened room and was sure the cat was sneering at him. Gloating that Alex was alone and the cat wasn't. Alex turned away sharply. As if he cared. He liked being alone. Preferred it.

He thought instead about the look on Toto's face as he'd gone into the house. Tom Tollinger was a few years younger than him, but they had known each other since grade school. While most people seemed to accept the new Alex, Toto never quite seemed to.

Toto came out of the house and Alex faced him once more, putting on a mask of worry and concern.

"Well?" he asked.

Toto shrugged. "Nothing seems out of place. Must have been a mistake. I didn't see any signs of a prowler."

"A prowler?" Alex shuddered, then laughed softly as if a thought had just occurred to him. "Oh, dear. Perhaps that was Heather. She was in the backyard about twenty minutes ago, catching a kitten."

Toto relaxed. "Yeah, that must have been it. A neighbor must have seen her and called it in on a cell phone. One of the drawbacks of a town this size. There's always someone watching you."

"Ah, but the caller meant well," Alex said. "Thanks goodness it was a false alarm."

"Yeah."

Toto shook Alex's hand as he thanked the policeman for his concern. Then he stood on the porch, watching until the squad car pulled away. Once it'd disappeared around the corner, Alex hurried inside to the phone and called his supervisor.

Casio answered on the first ring. "What the hell's going on?"

"Just a little accident," Alex replied.

"How little?"

He thought of Heather's petite frame and frowned. "Very little. A neighbor was in my yard looking for a cat."

"A cat? Not her cat?"

"Her cat. A cat. What's the difference?"

"I just want to make sure that we don't have a problem."

"We don't." It was Alex's turn to snap. "It was an accident."

"You're comfortable with this?" Casio asked.

Oh, man. Talk about paranoia. "It was just a neighbor looking for her cat," Alex said slowly. "It's the woman I went to school with. She's never given anyone trouble in her whole life and couldn't even if she tried."

"If you're sure."

"I'm positive. She's the last thing in the world I have to worry about."

"There you go, sweetie," Heather said to the kitten. "Getting hugged wasn't so bad, was it? I kind of like it myself."

Except there hadn't been much hugging lately, she thought with a sigh. She used to go out all the time, but after two or three dates, she'd know this guy or that one wasn't right for her and she'd break it off.

Slowly, over the past ten years, she'd pretty much run through the eligible bachelors in town, and there weren't too many new ones moving in. It got so that hugs were pretty rare, though she never stopped longing for them.

She got to her feet and shooed her two cats out of the room, along with the gloomies that wanted to fill her heart. Why was she suddenly so mopey tonight? She should be happy. She'd finally caught little… little…Bonnie—yes, that was a good name for her— and that was reason to celebrate. Maybe she'd have a lemonade before she went to bed. Henry stopped at the doorway with a plaintive meow.

"No, the new kitty can't come with us," Heather said. "She has to stay in here a little longer."

Henry looked ready to argue, but Heather just closed the door, leaning back against it with a frown. The note Alex had dropped was as bothersome as he was. Maybe it was some kind of paper that absorbed the moisture from the air and grew in size. Or maybe it was extrathick-and-heavy notepaper that weighed her down. Whatever, she was all too aware of it in her pocket.

"Should I take it over there?" she asked her cats as she wandered down the hall to the kitchen.

Neither of them expressed an opinion, either no more experienced with men than she was or they figured it was time she stood on her own two feet. She stopped at the screen door and looked over at Alex's house. A few lights were on so he was still up. But what if he had guests over? Or was in the shower? Or had guests in the shower? Her face blushed a bright hot red at the thought.

But it would be even worse if he was alone. He'd think she was just using the note as an excuse. He would think she was a poor pitiful old maid desperate to put a man in her life.

"No, I'll return it in the morning," she said and closed the inside door firmly. "I'll drop it off before I leave for Chicago for Karin's costume fitting. Or better yet, I'll put it in an envelope and drop it into his mailbox. Then I won't have to disturb him at all."

It was a good sensible plan, even if it did feel just a little bit old maidish. She flicked the lights off in the kitchen and walked through the semidarkness toward the living room. Of course, she had a right to be old maidish where Alex was concerned. He used to race across the seawall for goodness sake!

A knocking at the back door stopped her short, stopped her breath, too. Could it be Alex?

Her face burned suddenly, but it was cool compared to her heart which was racing so fast she surely would faint. Oh my goodness. Alex Waterstone coming over here? What could he want? What if he was as lonely as her and just wanted to spend the evening here?

This had never happened to her before. Panic gripped her. What was she supposed to do? Offer him a drink maybe.

Oh, no! She only had stuff like root beer and lemonade. Nothing exotic and sophisticated and intellectual. And her snack foods were animal crackers and ice cream. And what would they talk about?

Besides which, she was still in her napping kitty pajamas! She ran her hands down her sides. She couldn't—

Her hand stopped at the folded paper in her pajama pocket. The paper. That's all he was doing here. He'd come back for the paper. Her silly worries fell to the ground with a thud. What had she really feared? That he was suddenly overcome with passion for her? Get real, Heather Anne, she scolded herself.

She went over to the door and pulled it open. It wasn't Alex, though, it was Toto.

"Toto." Heather opened the screen door to let him in. "What are you doing here? Have you heard from Dorothy?" Her friend, who was also Toto's former girlfriend, had recently moved to Paris.

Toto just shook his head as he came inside. "No. But Penny and Brad promised to call after they've seen her."

"Lucky that Brad had that conference to go to in Paris or we wouldn't know how she was doing."

Poor Toto. He seemed lost since Dorothy had moved to Paris last week. Even more so since he'd rushed to the airport to say goodbye to her, only to get a flat tire and miss her flight.

"Anyway, I was going home after my shift." Toto stooped down to scratch the cats. "I saw your light on and decided to make sure everything was all right."

"I'm so glad you did," Heather said. "Everything's fine, but I can always use some company. Want some lemonade?"

"Sure." Toto straightened up and went over to the kitchen table. "I had a call to check out Alex's place this evening. I guess someone saw you in the yard and thought you were a prowler."

"Me?" She had started to pour some lemonade, but then stopped to stare at her friend. "My gosh. I'm so sorry. I hope that didn't cause any trouble."

"Nah. Alex didn't seem put out at all." Toto sat down. "I was surprised to hear you were over there, though. I always thought you were afraid of him."

How did they get on this subject? Heather fiddled around, pouring the lemonade carefully before bringing the glasses over to the table. Then she got out the animal crackers and sat down herself.

"I'm not afraid of him," she said brightly. "I don't know where you got that idea."

Toto reached for a handful of cookies. "Maybe because you used to practically faint if you had to talk to him."

"That's silly." She pulled a cookie out of the bag and concentrated on nibbling on its toes. "Besides, we're not in junior high anymore."

Why was Alex bombarding her life this evening? She had lived next door to him for almost a year now and she'd hardly been aware of him. Now, this evening, she couldn't seem to get away from him. She decided to take charge of the conversation, too. It wasn't as if Toto's life were in order.

"I think you should go to Paris," she told Toto.

He looked startled, stopping a gorilla cookie halfway to his mouth. "To Paris?"

"Sure," Heather said, warming to the idea. "Why not? You haven't taken a vacation in years. It would do you good." Plus maybe in a romantic place like Paris, he'd realize that he and Dorothy were meant for each other.

"I can't afford it," he said. "I just bought the house, you know."

And let the woman he should be sharing it with walk out of his life. "Come on, Toto," Heather said. "How much can it cost? Stay with Dorothy and let her show you the sights."

"But I'd need a passport. And probably shots."

"Maybe," Heather said. She wasn't exactly a seasoned traveler herself. A trip into Chicago was a big deal for her. "Ask at the travel agency."

"I don't know." He sighed and sat back in his chair. "Dorothy probably wouldn't want to see me anyway."

"Would you stop being so scared of everything?"

"I'm not scared of anything," he snapped. "And besides, you're a fine one to talk. When's the last time you did something without worrying for half a lifetime over it?"

"I do lots of things without worrying," she insisted.

"Catching stray cats doesn't count."

"I do other things, too."

"So name one."

She would, just to show him. Except she couldn't think of any offhand. "Maybe I don't want to."

"Maybe you can't."

Heather frowned at him. Why hadn't she noticed what a pest he could be? "Maybe I think this whole conversation is silly."

He leaned forward, an annoying gleam in his eye. "You do one really brave thing and I'll go to Paris if you want me to."

This was insane! "You'd let your future happiness depend on my bravery?" she asked.

"Isn't that showing how brave I am?"

"No, how crazy."

He got to his feet with a grin. "You never would take a dare, would you?"

She looked down at the animal cookies spilling from the bag, and chose a lion, popping it into her mouth. "I've taken lots of dares," she said though she couldn't presently think of any. "And I'll take this one. Better start working on that passport."

He actually looked surprised. "It has to be something good, not some wimpy thing."

"Stop putting restrictions on me," she said. "When I do it, I'll let you know."

"And I think it should have to do with Alex."

"I said no restrictions."

"I'm just clarifying what I mean by brave."

"You're just trying to weasel out of this," Heather said and got to her feet. "But I'll show you."

He laughed, obviously believing she was going to chicken out. "Sure you will. I know you, Heather." He leaned over and pecked at her cheek. "Take care. Call if you need anything."

Heather watched as Toto walked to his car and drove down the street. He was so sure she couldn't do anything brave concerning Alex. So positive. She was going to have to prove him wrong. For Dorothy's sake. For Toto's sake. For the sake of their future happiness together, she had to prove him wrong.

One really brave thing with Alex. How hard could that be?

Dorothy bit into her croissant with a sigh. She was having breakfast at a tiny café near her apartment. The buildings were full of history, the neighborhood was full of culture, and the café was filled with the most delectable smells. In the distance, through the early morning mist, she could see the Eiffel Tower, looming in the day's first shadows. And she even had a line on a job at little art gallery a few blocks from her.

So why wasn't she ecstatically happy?

"Dorothy!"

She looked up to see Penny weaving her way through the outdoor seating area. "Oh, Pen, it's so great to see you," Dorothy cried, getting to her feet to hug her friend. "Gosh, I can't believe you and Brad are really engaged."

"Sometimes I can't either," Penny said with a laugh as they sat down at Dorothy's table. "How have you been?"

"Just great," Dorothy said, conveniently ignoring the loneliness that followed her like a shadow. "It's everything I dreamed it would be and more. How's the conference?"

"I don't know. Brad had to go check in. I'm going to meet him later. I'm so glad you left a message at the hotel for me to meet you here. I've been dying to talk to you.'' Penny sat down at Dorothy's table, nodding as the waiter brought over coffee.

Once he was gone, Penny leaned forward. ''So, have you heard from Toto?''

''Toto?'' Dorothy didn't have to pretend confusion. ''Why would I hear from him?''

''He went after you the night you left,'' Penny told her. ''But he got to Chicago too late. Your plane was already gone.''

Dorothy didn't know what to think or feel or say. She put her croissant down carefully and tried to gather her thoughts. ''What did he want?'' she asked.

Penny shrugged. ''He said he wanted to say goodbye and wish you luck, but who knows what he really wanted.''

Good old Penny. Always trying to make everything right for everybody. Except sometimes she just couldn't, no matter how hard she tried.

''What else would he have wanted?'' Dorothy asked, her voice brisk enough to keep the hurt at bay. ''We've been friends for twenty years. I'm sure he does wish me well here.''

''There's lots of other things he might have wanted to say,'' Penny replied. ''I was hoping he would have called you since he missed your plane.''

But Dorothy just watched an old man riding his bike down the brick street, his basket filled with freshly baked bread. When he turned onto another street and disappeared from view, Dorothy turned back to her friend. She'd had enough time to know the truth.

''It's over,'' she told Penny. ''Or maybe it never was. If Toto and I were in love like you and Brad, we'd have known it ages ago. It was time for me to move on and this was the right place. I love my new life here.''

"Yes, but…" Penny sighed, a sad smile on her face. "I know. Everybody's got to find their own way. But I just want you to be as happy as I am.''

"And I will be," Dorothy assured her. "Just give me a little time to find the Jacques of my dreams.''

"But you and Toto are so perfect together," Penny wailed.

How perfect a couple could they be if they let an ocean come between them? "Jacques and I will be more perfect," Dorothy declared.

She only wished her heart believed it, too.

Chapter Three

Alex decided to run another mile, following the path around the lake instead of heading for home. It was early—the morning traffic had barely gotten started—and he had energy to burn. Along with some irritation.

That episode with Heather last night had been mildly amusing. A little diversion that should have put a lightly humorous end to the evening. Instead, he kept reliving it—or reliving parts of it—all night long. Everytime he fell asleep he was back in the garden, pulling his gun and almost shooting her.

The whole thing was crazy. He was a professional. He had never shot anybody accidentally, or the wrong person, or an innocent bystander. Yet in his dreams, he kept thinking he was in danger and then it would turn out to be Heather. Insane.

He passed the old boathouse and headed into the dense trees, the path weaving around old oaks and elms and maples. He'd always liked it here by the small lake on the edge of town, but the early morning was the best. There was no one around, the world was his.

He'd started coming here when he'd been twelve, after his dad died, finding the solitude a blessing. Every place else he'd gone then, people seemed to be watching him. Pitying him. Trying to take care of him. He'd hated it. He'd tried to tell them all that he was all right, but no one had listened. And that pity had stayed in everyone's eyes. So he'd done what his dad would have wanted—he gave them something to look at. He climbed everything in sight, trees, water towers, silos. He jumped from roofs and branches and windows. He drove down the steepest hills, raced around the sharpest curves and spun into the wildest turns until no one had known what to expect from him. It had been just what he'd wanted.

Maybe it had been the beginning of his undercover work, he thought with a smile as he followed the path around to the street. Or maybe it was his true nature taking over. Yeah, that was more like it. He'd always been a private person and so it was only natural that he choose a profession that let him stay private. He cut across the library parking lot to his street, slowing to a jog to cool down. More people were stirring now, but even at it's busiest, Chesterton was a sleepy little town. An easy place to fool.

Now why should that suddenly seem bothersome? He spotted his elderly neighbor getting her morning newspaper from the front sidewalk and waved as he turned into his drive.

He felt so much better. All that earlier nonsense was just tension about the upcoming job. Not that he was worried about it. No, it was the waiting for things to get rolling. He picked up his paper and went around the side of the house.

And ran smack into Heather.

"Ack!" she screamed and jumped about ten feet, clutching at her heart.

Alex reached out and grabbed her arms, afraid she was going to fall over. She didn't exactly. It was more like she crumpled slightly and he suddenly found himself holding her as she lay against his chest. His arms folded around her of their own accord—not that his brain disagreed. He couldn't have her collapse on his sidewalk, after all. But his heart continued to race, mocking his avowed good intentions. And his senses seemed overwhelmed by her faint scent of flowers.

"Gracious, I am so sorry," she said, pulling back from him. Her face was flushed and her voice unsteady.

He had the urge to pull her back into his arms, part of him not at all certain she wasn't about to faint. But the stronger part of him took a step back from her. To where the air was easier to breathe.

"Are you all right?" he asked. "I didn't trample you too badly?"

"I'm fine," she said though her voice still sounded strangled and her eyes seemed to be having a hard time meeting his. "I should have been watching where I was going."

He could feel the heat of her embarrassment even a few steps away and felt the irrational need to ease it. But what was irrational about it? She was a nice person, had never done anything to anybody. Easing her embarrassment was only a gentlemanly thing to do.

"How's the kitten this morning?"

An uncertain smile peeked out on her lips as she

looked up at him. "She's the sweetest thing. Still pretty scared but coming around." She seemed to take a deep breath, then rushed on. "Would you like to come see her sometime? She said she'd like to see you again."

"I...uh," he stammered.

Heather looked so damned fragile, so damned vulnerable, that he couldn't speak. Refusing would crush her, yet he couldn't afford to accept. He was a loner. Always was, always would be. To accept and let her believe otherwise would just hurt her more in the end. Damn the agency for thinking Chesterton was such a good idea.

He cleared his throat and hoped his words were gentle. "I'm afraid I—"

"Oh, of course not," she said quickly, those wide blue eyes darting away from his again. "I wasn't thinking straight. You're much too busy."

"It's just that I'm going to be traveling a lot," he told her. "Another professor and I have been discussing rhyming couplets in Shakespeare and may do a paper on it. We'll need to get together a lot for the collaboration."

"Sure. Of course. It was just a silly thought anyway." There was something in her voice that belied her words and tore at his heart. "Actually I just came by to return this. You dropped it yesterday."

She shoved a small piece of paper into his hand. It was the address for the gambling operation's headquarters.

He just stared down at it, his stomach churning. Damn. How could he have been so careless? This kind of mistake could have dire consequences for him and his partners. Where had his mind been? He had better be more careful.

He closed his hand around the paper. That's exactly what he would be from now on—more careful. Extremely careful. Extraordinarily careful. He would take this as a warning that he had been letting his edge slip and he would force himself to be more attentive.

"Thanks," he said with deliberate lightness. "I'd never locate my Shakespeare colleague without this."

"We wouldn't want that." She edged around him slightly. "Well, I need to be going. I'll see you around."

"Yes. Of course."

But she was gone before he barely got the words out, scurrying across his driveway and through her side door as if she were being pursued. The world was suddenly silent. No, it was filled with sound—the chirping of the birds, the distant sound of traffic and rustling of the wind in the trees. But they felt more empty than anything. Mocking sounds of a world filled with contentment.

What nonsense! He must have inhaled auto fumes, or been splashed by a strain of lake water that caused hallucinations.

He yanked open his back door and the first thing his gaze stopped at was the light of his security system. It was blinking at him. Damn. Not again.

He walked over to the security panel. Someone had been at the back door three minutes ago. Heather. After resetting the system, he went over to the phone and dialed the number.

Casio answered. "What the hell is going on?"

"Nothing," Alex snapped. "I'm fine. Everything's fine. The system's too sensitive."

"Too sensitive? You've lived there for ages and it rarely goes off. Now it's gone off twice in twelve hours."

"Look, nothing's wrong," Alex repeated. "I'll be leaving for Chicago in a few hours."

Heather Anne, she told herself as she fluffed the skirt of Karin's costume, you are an absolute, total failure.

She hadn't accomplished her brave deed. She hadn't even made a start. Yeah, she'd given Alex back his note and had invited him over, but she had made a fool of herself in the process.

Thanks goodness she had to go to Chicago to do a fitting on Karin's Oz Festival costume. With luck and all the costumes Heather was making, she wouldn't run into Alex for the next three centuries.

Heather sat back on her heels and frowned at the Glinda the Good Witch costume. "It doesn't fit as well as it did last time," she said. "It looks tight around the waist."

Karin looked down at her stomach. "Can you let it out?"

"Sure, but do you think we need to?" Heather asked. "Maybe you just had a big lunch. You know, you shouldn't eat that hospital food."

Karin laughed, but it didn't sound as if there was much humor in it. "Don't I wish it was that simple," she said and sank into a nearby chair. "I'm afraid it's little longer lasting than a big lunch of bad food. Nine months longer lasting."

"Nine months?" Heather repeated, stunned. Could she have misunderstood? "You're pregnant?"

"Surprised, huh?" Karin made a face. "Didn't think

I was human enough to fall for some jerk's sweet talking, did you?''

"No, that's not what I meant." A baby! How wonderful! But Heather took in Karin's drooped shoulders and the shadows under her eyes. "I take if you aren't as excited about the idea as I would be. How does the dad feel?''

"Dad? What dad?" Karin said. "He denies even being there that night.''

"Oh, Karin, what a bummer.'' No wonder she was depressed. "If there's anything I can do, just tell me. Anything at all.''

Karin's lips twisted into a bit of a smile as she got to her feet. "Well, there is one thing, besides not telling anyone just yet," she said.

"Sure. Just name it.''

"Let the costume out, will you? My mom is so proud that I'm grand marshall of the Oz festival she's about to burst. Can't have me not fitting into my costume now, can we?''

Heather got to her feet and hugged Karin. "You got it, girl. One maternity Glinda costume coming up.''

Heather worked on the costume for another hour or so, then Karin left to check on a patient she was operating on the next day. It wasn't until Heather was back on the expressway that she realized Karin's news had driven all thought of her foolishness with Alex from her mind for a while. Long enough for the embarrassment to fade and excitement over Karin's news to take its place. A baby. Karin was so lucky. Having a baby would be the most wonderful thing ever.

Heather awoke from her thoughts to realize that traffic was slowed ahead of her. It looked like a truck had stalled in her lane and the tow trucks were blocking the two other lanes. Nothing she could do but wait. She frowned and tapped the steering wheel nervously. She hated driving in heavy traffic—people cutting in and out, trucks breathing down her neck, road debris appearing out of nowhere. All around her, accidents were waiting to happen. And then she'd be the one in need of rescue.

The traffic inched forward. She glanced up at the green-and-white exit signs stretched over the highway. How unbelievably eerie. The next exit was for Poplar, the street that was on Alex's piece of paper.

Traffic had come to a complete standstill, but the exit ramp leading to Alex's friend's house was empty and beckoning. Tempting. All that room to drive. Why not? She could find a street that ran parallel to the expressway and get back on once she had passed the stalled truck.

Heather swung into the next lane and onto the off-ramp. It had to be a safe neighborhood if Alex's friend lived there. It would be fine. Nothing would happen. Except with her luck, Alex would be outside and see her. Her heart practically stopped at that thought.

But so what if he was? This was the new Heather, the one in search of brave deeds. She didn't care if Alex did see her. Not that this would be her brave deed, but it would be bravery practice.

It sounded good, but as she drove on, her hands started to sweat. What if her car broke down and she had to go to his friend's house to ask for help? Or if she got in an accident? Or witnessed a crime?

Her heart practically stopped. This was the dumbest thing she'd ever done. Absolutely, without a doubt, unquestionably the most idiotic, harebrained thing she'd ever thought of. Bravery practice, indeed!

She would turn around and get back on the express-way. Quickly, before fate had a chance to make a fool of her. All she had to do was find a place to turn around. A driveway. An alley. A side street.

Palms sweating, breathing hard, Heather gripped the steering wheel tighter and looked slowly around her. The neighborhood was run-down, to put it kindly. It had once been a commercial strip with businesses thriving behind those boardedup windows. But that obviously hadn't been anytime recent. It had taken more than one or two winters' worth of snow and ice to wear all the paint off the doorways. And more than two summers of blistering heat to make the wood trim cracked and dried.

There might be apartments above some of these old stores, but this was not the place an English professor would live. She must have remembered the address wrong. Or there was more than one Poplar Street in Chicago. The thought was only mildly reassuring. She might not be in danger from more Alex embarrassment, but she certainly didn't feel safe. She would just turn around and get back to the expressway, regardless of the traffic tieup.

There, up ahead. There was a side street. Up ahead where those men were standing.

Alex walked slowly across the small gravel parking lot and away from the old storefront. Feet shuffling, shoulders slumped. Hopefully, looking like a guy who gambled every last cent and then some. Not an under-cover federal agent with a tiny camera hidden in his tie tack.

With a weary sigh—you never knew who was watching—Alex shuffled over to the fence at the back of the lot and leaned on the top, staring in at the cars parked in the secure lot. A mangy-looking brown-and-white cat moved cautiously between them, watching the lot for signs of danger.

Alex smiled slightly. Good thing Heather wasn't here. She'd be over the fence and after the cat, the hell with the investigation.

His smile faded into a frown. Now where had that thought come from? He went back to his federal agent train of thought and took a few pictures of the lot, not that he expected anything of them, but you never knew.

Things were going great in the investigation. Both he and Casio had gotten into the illegal gambling den. He didn't know how Casio had done, but Alex had lost several thousand dollars, as planned, and taken a couple dozen photos. If he got no nibbles from loan sharks, he'd come back in a few days and lose even more. Sooner or later, he'd get offered the loan and they'd be deeper into the operation. Then the real plans could be implemented.

"What you doing down here, slumming?"

Alex turned. The man was well dressed and had the aura of a professional about him. Professional what, though?

"You look more like a Vegas kind of guy," the man went on.

Alex shrugged and touched the button on his coat. "Too far away to stay in touch. And the riverboats are filled with seniors playing the quarter slots. I'm looking for real action." He thought maybe he could risk pushing just a little more. "And someplace a little freer with the credit."

He got no response, just a hard stare. Then the man

looked away, gazing at the cars in the secure lot as if they were rare and beautiful sculptures to be admired.

"You feeling lucky?" the man asked after a moment.

Alex licked his lips, a man on the edge yet still trying to maintain his facade of macho pride. "All I need is a little seed money. Then let me roll them bones and I'll be hitting sevens and elevens the rest of my life."

"Seed money ain't free." The man looked Alex up and down, no doubt appraising his suit and tie, shoes and shirt. He wouldn't know how carefully this outfit had been put together to give just the right image, but he would know what it was worth.

"Hey, you need money to make money," Alex said, brushing off the warning. "And I'll only need it for a little bit. Just until I make my big score."

"Yeah, sure." The man shifted position. "You got any ID?"

Alex gave him his driver's license and two credit cards. The man pulled out a pocket computer and copied the data into it before returning them. Alex touched the suitcoat button a few more times.

"I got an office in back," the man said. "Come around in a half hour."

"Great. Sure. Thanks."

Alex was smiling as he pocketed his IDs. The man didn't bother to reply and just turned and left, but it wasn't like Alex was looking for a buddy.

Alex walked slowly back across the parking lot, keeping his elation under wraps. This was going just as they planned. The goons would be checking up on him in a matter of minutes and they'd find out all about Alex Waterstone III. Well, not all. Alex allowed himself a small smile. But they'd get enough to realize the potential there.

Damn, but this was great.

Alex's gaze wandered over the street as his hand in his pants pocket changed the film cassette in the tiny camera. Under cover of his handkerchief, he switched the three cassettes to his coat pocket and eased up on his shuffle slightly, going more for nervous pacing. He was, after all, waiting for his loan to be approved. He was probably being watched and had to play his part to perfection.

He wasn't the only one playing a part, though. Fitz came wandering over, dressed in jeans and a sweat-shirt. He was moving casually, then stopped, his back to Alex, as he appeared to try to light a cigarette. Alex just continued to walk by him, but Fitz pulled up behind him, jabbing a small gun into Alex's side.

"Hey!" Alex cried.

"Hands up." Fitz shoved the gun a little harder into Alex's side. "And mouth shut."

While Alex did as he was told, Fitz pulled Alex's wallet from his pocket, rifled through and took his few credit cards and the couple of dollars Alex had left. He tossed the empty wallet to the ground and reached into Alex's coat pocket, slipping out the film cassettes before waving his gun at Alex's watch.

"Hand that over too, big—"

But the next thing Alex knew, Fitz was reeling, falling to the ground. Alex spun around. A woman holding a large purse was kicking Fitz's dropped gun farther away from him. No, it wasn't kicking—nudging maybe, or inching—but timidly moving it away like it might go off if she really touched it.

It couldn't be!

Good lord, it was!

"Heather?" Alex grabbed up the gun himself. "What the hell are you doing?"

Getting ready to faint might be one answer. Her face was white, her eyes were wide and her hands were trembling. She was clutching her purse as if it were a lifeline.

"Are you okay?" he asked.

She was staring down at Fitz—still on the ground, shaking his head slowly and seeming dazed—then she looked back up at Alex. "You're not going to shoot him, are you?"

He just frowned at her and then at the gun in his hand. "I'm not planning on shooting anybody," he told her.

"Make him give back your stuff before you shoot him," she said, her eyes on him as she dug around in her purse blindly. Her voice was thready, but she seemed to still have her wits about her. Unfortunately.

"I'm not going to shoot him." He couldn't believe this! But he had to play along or blow both his cover and Fitz's. "Hey, fella. Give me back my credit cards."

Fitz handed him the small stack of credit cards he'd taken, then started getting to his feet slowly. Playing it cautiously, Alex knew. He pocketed the cards.

"The rest of the stuff too," Heather said, still searching in her purse. "He took something from your coat pocket."

Alex looked at her. Maybe it would be better if she fainted. He'd thought the film cassette exchange had gone so well and now she was going to screw it up.

"No, he didn't," Alex said. "He wanted my watch but I hadn't taken it off."

Fitz was on his feet now, standing a few feet away, trying to look as contrite as a caught mugger might, but mostly he looked confused. Alex knew exactly how he felt.

"I was sure…" Heather began, then pulled out a little vial from her purse. "Aha!"

She cracked the vial open and held it near her nose, taking a deep breath. Her eyes widened and she shuddered a little, then seemed to realize they were both staring at her.

"Oh, it doesn't matter," she said to Alex and slipped the vial into her pocket. She pulled a cellular phone from her purse. "You just watch him and I'll call the police—"

"No," Alex said quickly as if he'd gotten a whiff of the smelling salts too. Actually both he and Fitz might have said it together, but he ignored that little fact and frowned at Heather. "We need to get out of here."

She frowned back. "But—"

Geez, police was all they needed. As if they weren't attracting enough attention as it was. He took Heather's hand and pulled her back a step from Fitz.

"He could have accomplices here," Alex said and glanced around them nervously. "We'd better just go."

Heather started looking around nervously also, and her hold on the purse got tighter. He thought maybe her face went a shade paler but it was already so pale, it was hard to tell. He felt a twinge of guilt at increasing her fear, but hell, she had screwed everything up for them!

Damn. That bit of knowledge didn't help. He felt

like a heel. Like an absolute crud. He tossed Fitz's gun
into a nearby garbage can—where Fitz could retrieve
it—and pulled Heather toward her car.

"Come on," he said.

Chapter Four

"Are you sure you're all right?" Heather pulled into her driveway. "I can take you over to the emergency room."

"I don't need a doctor," Alex said. "I'm not the one who's been sniffing smelling salts the whole way home."

"I was not," she cried. "I just sniffed them once because I wondered how long they stayed potent."

"You should have let me drive."

"You couldn't. You'd been mugged."

"Well, you were about to pass out."

His voice was sharp and terse—she was hoping it was just a reaction to being attacked—but she really didn't care. Much as she would prefer to avoid him, she couldn't have left him there, being mugged. She still could not believe that it had occurred as she had been driving by. It was just like old times—whenever she was around Alex, things happened. She turned off the ignition and glanced his way. He looked all right, it was true, but how could she tell? What if he had internal injuries?

"We should have gone to the hospital in Chicago," she said. "I should have insisted."

"And I should have agreed," Alex said with a quiet intensity as he unbuckled his seat belt. "So you could be checked over."

"I'm fine."

"So am I."

It was all macho nonsense, Heather knew. He was embarrassed about being mugged. Or embarrassed that she had overpowered the mugger with her sewing bag. Which was about as silly as it got; she was still shivering from the whole idea. She undid her seat belt and got out of the car. Hurrying around to his side, she took his arm as he got out.

"What are you doing now?" he asked.

She ignored his question. She wasn't sure what that new element she heard in his voice was—impatience, astonishment, confusion—but it was not going to stop her.

"I'm helping you out of the car," she said and leaned past him to close the car door. "You're sure you don't feel any pain? Any soreness? Are you light-headed?"

"Heather, I am fine," he said. Slowly. Enunciating every word carefully and distinctly. "There is absolutely nothing wrong with me."

This time she couldn't ignore that something in his voice, but she could refuse to put a name to it. And refuse to let it bother her. She was doing what she had to, what was right to do. She was doing for Alex what she would have done for anyone that she had seen in trouble.

"Come on inside and sit down," she said, still holding his arm. She was trying hard to remember something—anything—she might have read about internal injuries. "I'll make us some dinner."

He stopped walking. Or maybe he'd never started. Heather wasn't sure. She did see that he was frowning at her though.

"I really appreciate your help, but I'd much rather just go home. By myself."

Heather wanted to back down. Certainly she'd rather he go home, but she also knew that she couldn't let him. No matter how uncomfortable she was around him. "No," she said. "What happens if you faint or start to bleed or hallucinate?"

"Look, Heather—"

Why were men so stupidly stubborn? "No, you look. I was scared to death that mugger, or his accomplices, was following us. Well, I got you this far. I am not going to leave you in your house to have some kind of post-traumatic stress attack."

She expected an argument, another denial, but what she got was a dumbfounded stare. "You thought we were still in danger?" he asked.

She wished she was brave enough to hit him, to just wallop him a good one and lay him out flat. Was the fact that he had been with her supposed to keep her from being afraid?

"You know me, always a chicken," was all she said though. "Come on. Let's go inside."

He didn't move, just stood there in the middle of her driveway frowning at her. "What were you doing there anyway?" he asked.

She felt her cheeks burn. ''Just driving by,'' she said quickly. ''Now just come inside, will you? Once you're sitting down and relaxing, we can talk all you want.''

He must have agreed, for although he didn't say anything, he did walk with her into her house. Victoria and Henry came running to greet them, but Heather settled Alex in the recliner before fussing over them. They were more than willing to follow her into the kitchen.

''What an adventure we had,'' she told them as she refilled their water dish. ''I actually knocked a mugger down.''

Victoria was unimpressed but Henry rubbed against Heather's legs sympathetically. Heather picked the little cat up and hugged it. Now that she was home, everything seemed to be catching up to her.

''I thought I was going to throw up about ten times,'' she told Henry. ''I was so scared.''

''Then why'd you do it?''

Heather spun around. Alex was in the kitchen doorway, leaning against the wood trim and looking puzzled. He was so breath-stoppingly handsome with his broad shoulders and narrow hips that she felt her nerves all tense up again.

''What are you doing up?'' she scolded. She needed more breathing space. Putting Henry down, she shooed Alex back into the living room. ''Next thing you know, you're going to be passed out on the floor and I'm going to have to find another tube of smelling salts and it'll turn out that they're all dried up and no good, but you'll have an allergic reaction to them anyway and I'll have to call the paramedics who won't be able to get you through the door because your shoulders are too wide.''

She stopped in horror with Alex staring at her. He looked confused. She hadn't really said what she thought she said, had she? Only a total idiot—or a woman who normally got love letters written in crayon by five-year-olds—would let her mouth ramble on like that. What must he think of her?

She tried to look more professional, more competent, and waved him back toward the recliner. ''Please sit down,'' she said. ''I just need to check on Bonnie and then I'll make us some dinner.''

''Who's Bonnie?'' he asked, neither sitting nor looking like he was going to pass out.

''The kitten we rescued the other night. That's what I named her.''

''Oh. So, are you going to go socialize her now?''

Heather took a step back. Lordy, but he was tall. Her mouth went dry. ''I was going to check to make sure she was okay and give her clean water,'' she said. ''Once I had dinner started, I was going to work with her a little.''

''I'm not that hungry,'' he said. ''Let's go see Bonnie.''

''I really should...'' She stopped and sighed. She really should insist he sit down. But then she should have insisted they go to an emergency room in Chicago. Or to the clinic here in town. Insisting wasn't her specialty. Maybe she could bargain.

''All right. We'll check on her quickly and then you'll go sit down while I start dinner.'' She led him down the hall to the back bedroom. At least this time that he was following her down her hallway, she was dressed.

Heather guessed she should be glad that he didn't seem quite so angry anymore. She opened the bedroom door, then closed it after them. It felt very scary to be closed up in the room with him. But deliciously scary somehow. She didn't know what to think.

"So, how does this work?" he asked.

Thank goodness he wasn't afflicted with the same mental inertia. Heather went over to the cage. Bonnie was just waking up, stretching her tiny legs and flexing her little feet. Every time Heather saw the kitten she was overcome with love for the tiny creature. And felt a slight sliver of sadness that she had no one but her cats to give that love to. No one really special.

What was with her today? she scolded herself. You'd think she was the one who had been mugged. Kneeling on the floor, she opened the cage and reached in for the kitten. Bonnie backed away from her hand, but Heather got her out and cuddled the kitten up by her chest.

"I just take her out," she said. "And pet her until she purrs and talk to her softly so that she sees she doesn't have to be afraid of me."

"Sounds easy."

"Want to try?" Heather asked. "Here, sit down and I'll give her to you."

"No," Alex said. His voice was sharp.

She stopped, surprised at his tone. "No?"

"No to the sitting down." He had softened his tone, as he came over and took Bonnie from Heather's hands. "Not no to the kitten."

He held the kitten to his chest and petted her softly, breathing soft little words of reassurance into her fur. He'd scarcely begun before Bonnie was purring loud enough to be heard the next block over.

And the more he stroked the kitten, the more Heather's stomach tightened. The more she tasted worry and fear. What was wrong with her? Heather asked herself. Just watching him with the little animal shook her heart and almost made her tremble. Heather had to look away. And then reality—and sanity—returned.

"What do you mean 'no to the sitting down'?" she asked.

He looked up from petting Bonnie. "Just what I said. I'm not sitting down. I'm on a standing-up strike."

What was he talking about? "Why?"

"Because you won't answer my question," he said. "Every time I ask you why you rescued me, you avoid answering."

This was nuts. She got to her feet and took Bonnie back, giving her a hug and kiss before putting the kitten back in the cage. No need to take out her irritation with Alex on a little innocent kitten.

"I didn't answer because I thought it was obvious."

"So humor me."

"You needed help, so I gave it." She knew she sounded curt, but didn't care as she pulled open the bedroom door, holding it for him to leave the room. "What's the big mystery?"

He walked out slowly and she winced. She was the world's worst nurse, letting her own worries distract her. She hurried up next to him and took his arm. "I really would like you to sit down now," she said. "I'll pour us some iced tea…no, the caffeine might be bad for you. And so would alcohol. Maybe some ice water."

"Most people wouldn't, you know," he said.

''Wouldn't what?'' He didn't look pale, or sound weak, but that didn't mean anything. ''Wouldn't have stopped? Of course they would have. Would you rather sit in the kitchen? It's nice and cool in there.''

She led him into the kitchen and he sat down, though she wasn't sure he was aware of it. His face was creased with a frown and his eyes seemed not to be seeing the daisy print wallpaper that he was staring at.

''Most people don't give a damn about anyone else and would never put themselves in danger for someone.''

''How did you ever get so cynical?'' She took two glasses from the cabinet—ones with big letters of the alphabet dancing all over the sides—and filled then with ice and water and handed him a glass.

''My kids gave them to me as a Christmas present last year,'' she informed him.

''Your kids?''

''My class. I teach kindergarten.''

''Of course.'' He seemed to shake himself. ''I was just wondering why you weren't married with a houseful of kids to take care of and got confused.''

She froze, just staring at him. ''You're hallucinating. Oh lord, what do I do now?''

But he just started to laugh, and that alarmed her even more. Hallucinations. Hallucinations. What did one do for hallucinations? Starve a cold, feed a fever. Rest, ice and elevate for a sprain. Floss every day. Why hadn't she paid better attention during all those first-aid courses?

''Are you dizzy?'' she cried as she rushed around the table. ''How many fingers am I holding up?''

''I'm fine. Really. No need to panic.''

''Panic? Don't tell me not to panic,'' she said as she

reached out to feel his forehead. "I clobbered a mugger today. I'm allowed to panic when someone's going to collapse in my kitchen."

But as she got to his side, he was standing up and her silly feet took her right smack into him. His arms folded around her as if they always did so, and then he was holding her up.

"I'm not going to collapse," he told her softly.

"I think I might."

Her legs didn't seem to want to hold her, or else they had turned to cooked spaghetti and weren't able to. His arms were so strong and it was so nice to have someone else doing the supporting. But this was Alex! Even so, her head lay against his chest and her eyes closed.

"You've had quite a day," he said, his breath tickling the hair on the top of her head.

"I hit somebody." She shivered and burrowed deeper into his arms. His hold tightened. "And I thought you were going to get killed."

"You were very brave."

He was just saying that to be nice. She knew this wouldn't count as her brave deed; she'd been too scared. "I almost fainted about ten times," she admitted. "I wasn't really checking the potency of the smelling salts."

"You should have let me drive."

"You had reason to be hurt. I was just being my usual chicken self."

"Would you stop putting yourself down?" he said.

She looked up just as he was bending down and it happened. Somehow he was kissing her. Or was she kissing him? Whatever it was, whoever was doing what to whomever, it shouldn't be happening! Her stomach tensed, but then his lips were so soft, so soothing, so scrumptious that she couldn't resist. She'd never had a kiss like this before, never had one that made her feel so alive and precious and desirable. She raised herself up on her tiptoes just slightly so that she could better feel those magical lips against hers.

As she raised herself up, his arms tightened around her and the warm, wondrous, absolutely terrifying feeling spread from her lips to cover her whole body. Her knees felt treacherously weak and wobbly and her head felt light. She thought briefly about getting out her smelling salts, but this was a different feeling. One she liked and didn't want to chase away. One she—

Alex was letting go of her and the world was coming back. She felt unsettled, as if she'd just stepped off an upside-down roller coaster. What in the world was she doing?

She took a step back, unable to look clearly at him. This was not her brave deed. This was insanity.

"I think I'd better go," he said.

"But what about dinner?" Heather asked.

She looked so lost and helpless, like that kitten she'd caught, that Alex felt like a complete heel. He was suddenly the mugger and she was the muggee. What was the matter with him? Why had he gone ahead and kissed her? Why had he even come into her house? He should have known better.

Why had she ever stumbled onto that scene today? If she hadn't, then none of this would have happened. He didn't need this kind of complication right now. Hell, not just right now, he didn't need it ever.

"I think I should go home and lie down," he said

and edged toward the back door. "I'll feel better there."

"Are you sure you should be alone?" she asked.

The knife went in deeper and twisted. This wasn't her fault. It was his. He had kissed her. He had gotten her out of that street scene. He had dropped that stupid paper in her kitchen last night that had given her the address. Now it was his job to let her down easy—but to minimize his future involvement. It was time for a well-placed lie.

"Uh, I won't be alone," he said.

"Oh?" Then her face turned bright red and her eyes took on a hurt look that would have broken his heart if he'd let it. "Oh."

Damn. He couldn't do it. "No, no, that's not what I meant." Though it was exactly what he'd intended. "I mean that I won't be alone because some students are supposed to drop by. I'm heading the athletic tutoring program this year and some of my student tutors are coming by."

"Oh. I see."

The red in her face had paled to just a rosy glow. A tempting, tantalizing glow that—

He definitely needed to get out of here and now. "Well, thanks for everything," he said, making his way closer to the door. "I imagine I'll see you around."

"Don't let your students keep you up too late," she said. "You need your rest."

He nodded reluctantly. "Yeah. You too. You had a trying day, too."

"It was kind of exciting," she said. "Now that it's all over, I mean."

Geez, that was all he needed. "Just don't go to liking that kind of excitement too much,'' he snapped. "That was really a pretty tame mugger.''

"And you might not always be there to pick up the gun,'' she added.

"That, too.'' The idea worried him and the knowledge that it did worried him even more. "Well, I'd really better go.''

He got outside, but the evening air wasn't sharp and cool enough to clear his thoughts. Why, he had no idea. And didn't want to know either.

He hurried across the yard to his own house, unlocked his door, and went inside, pausing only then to breathe a sigh of relief in the cool conditioned air.

"Have a nice dinner?'' Casio asked.

Alex's blood froze and it seemed like centuries before he was able to breathe. "What the hell are you doing in here?''

How had he let his guard down like that? He should have sensed Casio before he opened the door. Regardless of his security system, he should have known someone was here. It was his job to know.

His mind had just been so muddled because of Heather that he wasn't thinking clearly or reacting properly. This time it was only his supervisor who had surprised him. Next time it could be someone dangerous. Still further reason that he had to keep Heather out of his life.

"What am I doing here? I'm your supervisor and I'm supposed to keep an eye on you,'' Casio replied. "Remember?''

Alex let the fire go from his blood and relaxed. Just another day at the office and he and Casio were going to discuss how things went. No big deal. Unless he made it so.

"Yeah, right." Alex walked across the room to his sofa and flopped down on it. "It's just been a long day and I'm a little tired. Need to catch a couple of Zs."

"How did it go inside?" Casio asked.

"Great. Just great. I lost big and got approached by a backer willing to finance my run of luck."

"And?"

Alex frowned. "And I need to finalize things tomorrow. I got...uh...sidetracked and didn't get it finished." How much did Casio know? And how much did Alex have to confess?

"You mean when you got rescued?" Casio asked.

Damn. Alex had known he would have to explain but he had somehow hoped he'd have time to come up with a sensible explanation. Time when he didn't have to look at the smirk on Casio's face. "Yeah. When I got rescued."

"So, what's with her?" Casio asked. "She's your neighbor, right? A cute little thing."

Cute little thing? Alex's first reaction was to come out swinging. Who the hell did Casio think he was talking about? But that was crazy and Alex knew it. There was nothing between him and Heather. They were neighbors who barely knew each other. No reason for him to get defensive.

"Yeah," Alex said. "She saw me and thought I needed help."

"Fitz said she swings a mighty purse," Casio said.

Alex shrugged. "Yeah. He's okay, isn't he? I thought he was just playing it up."

"He's fine. But what's going on with you and the neighbor?"

Alex got up from the sofa, suddenly unable to sit still. "What's going on with us? Nothing. She just happened to be driving by and saw Fitz and me and jumped to the wrong conclusion. I hope it didn't screw things up too much.'' He started into the kitchen, then stopped. ''Want something to drink?''

''Nah.'' Casio got to his feet and followed Alex into the kitchen though. ''Actually the woman was a real bonus.''

Alex paused, his hand on the refrigerator door and his breath suddenly stuck in his throat. ''What do you mean?''

''You two made a great picture today. It made you look like someone who's hanging on by his finger-nails.''

''I was doing okay in that regard on my own,'' Alex said.

''Yeah, you were doing fine. But when you add this little sweetie pie coming along to rescue you, it really iced it. She looked really, really concerned. Anybody watching would know it wasn't a setup.''

''It was an accident,'' Alex said sharply and yanked open the refrigerator door. ''And it won't happen again.''

''If they did any checking on you, they'd figure she was your girlfriend.''

Alex snatched a can of soda from the fridge and slammed the door shut. ''She's not—''

''We need to let them keep thinking that,'' Casio said. ''Even if they should come out and take a look for themselves.''

Alex could not believe what Casio was saying. ''Things could get dangerous. It's a bad idea to have a civilian involved.''

''She's not really involved,'' Casio said. ''She's more like—'' he shrugged ''—window dressing.''

Alex didn't like where this was going. Not at all. "Windows get broken," he pointed out.

"It's not like we're going to actively involve her," Casio said. "But if she wants to rescue you and fuss over you, so be it. There's probably more danger in her crossing the street than in getting peripherally involved in this."

There was danger and there was danger. Alex didn't want Heather involved in this thing in any way. Not at all. He didn't want to have to watch out for her. Or worry that someone going after him might get her by mistake. Or...

Or what? That he'd get caught in that soft smile of hers?

Nope. That was one thing that would never happen. Never.

Chapter Five

Heather was relieved when Alex left. Okay, so there was an awful ache in the region of her heart, but it was just because she'd screwed up another chance to be brave. Just as her reaction to Alex's kiss had been because of all the stress of tangling with a mugger. Alex Waterstone was the last man on earth she wanted to kiss her. And if her crazy heart was screaming she was a liar, it only went to show how terribly stressful the day had been.

Heather much preferred her quiet life to the uproar that accompanied Alex everywhere. She didn't like uproar. She didn't need uproar. To be honest, uproar scared her. She kept telling herself that all evening until she went to bed.

She got up the next morning as soon as it was light and started chores. It was too early for any sane person to be up, so she went outside in her pajamas—these had teddy bears on them—and started filling the two birdbaths in her backyard. After that, she set the hose to watering the dogwood that shaded the near birdbath and walked back toward the house.

And saw him.

Alex was coming around the side of his house in his running clothes, looking like something out of her favorite dream. Those long muscled legs, his arms so strong, and those lips that had tasted better than she ever could have imagined.

And here she was in her pajamas again! She felt her whole body go hot, and then numb. Not that her pajamas were the slightest bit revealing. They were just a no-nonsense set of cotton shirt and shorts. No lacy peekaboo holes or fluttery thin straps that men found attractive. Even so, that same knot appeared in the pit of her stomach. No, her fear of him certainly didn't have anything to do with the past or his actions now, as her neighbor. It was all inside her, her reaction to him. She knew she should run, but her feet wouldn't move. This was her chance to win Toto's dare.

"Hi," she called out. "You're up early."

He looked surprised to see her. "So are you."

His voice sounded tight. Maybe he hadn't slept well. Maybe some injury had been—

"Are you all right?" she asked quickly. "No ill effects from yesterday?"

"Depends on what you mean by ill effects," he said. "No aches and pains."

He was trying for a joke, she knew, so she laughed. He didn't seem to have it in him to join her, though. Now that she looked closer, his eyes looked tired, too, and there were little worry wrinkles around his mouth. What if—

No! She was not going to worry about him! That wasn't part of Toto's challenge. She just had to be brave and that's what she was doing. Just in case though, she backed away a step or two.

"Well, I hope your 'no aches and pains' don't keep you from having a good run," she said brightly. "I really admire anyone with the discipline to jog regularly. I keep thinking I should, but I probably couldn't get halfway down the block without having an asthma attack."

"I didn't know you had asthma," he said. "Getting tangled up with a mugger yesterday was probably the worst thing for you."

She just made a face, not liking the fact that she'd trapped herself in the corner like that. "It wasn't a problem, really. I haven't had too many attacks lately." Like none in the past ten years. "It was worse when I was a kid."

He frowned, and she felt a tingle all the way down to her toes. Was his reaction concern?

"But it could come back," he said, sounding half angry for some reason. "Any kind of stress could trigger another attack."

"Oh, I doubt it," she said. She didn't know what was going on, but tried to make light of it all. "Besides, I don't have time for an asthma attack just now. School starts next week and I still have a lot of costumes to finish for the festival."

"You're making your Oz costume?"

"Mine?" She just laughed. He really didn't know her, did he? Somehow it released her from his spell. "Gracious, I don't dress up myself. I make costumes for other people. I'm making a Glinda the Good Witch costume for Karin Spencer. You remember her, don't you? She's going to be one of the grand marshalls this year."

"So I heard. Quite an honor."

"She's really done well. She's a surgeon at Rush Presbyterian Hospital in Chicago." Heather stopped. "But you've done really well, too. A professor at a big university. I wonder why they've never asked you."

Alex appeared startled at the idea. "Fine with me if they haven't. Really. It's not something I'd want to do."

"But you've accomplished just as much as Karin." He had to have been hurt by the slight, even if he was pretending he wasn't. "I'm going to talk to the committee. Since Owen Philips has to have bypass surgery, they're looking for a new co-grand marshall to partner with Karin and you would be perfect. They'll just do a quick background check—"

"No," Alex said quickly. It had to be hurt that was making his voice sound annoyed. "Really. I'd rather that you didn't."

"Oh, don't be so shy," Heather said. "Think of how proud your mother would be."

"Well, that's part of it." He paused and took a deep breath. "I'm not sure my mother would be able to come to the festival this year and I'd hate for her to miss it." He glanced down the street and then at his watch. "Wow, look at the time. I'd better get going or I'll run into lots of traffic."

"Better than it running into you," she said.

He stared at her a long moment. And then he laughed, as if suddenly realizing she'd been making a joke. "Well, have a nice day," he said and took a few steps backward before turning and jogging off down the block.

Heather pulled down the gravel drive and parked her car. Penny's grandmother—her name was Emma but all Penny's friends called her Aunty Em—came out on the porch. She still had a slight limp from her hip surgery, but was no longer using her cane.

"Hi, Aunty Em," Heather called as she got out of the car. "You're looking great. Hear anymore from Penny and Brad?"

"They're having a great time in Paris, but she's fretting over me being here alone. You'd think I was a two-year-old."

Heather just laughed as she climbed up on the porch and gave the older woman a hug. "Don't get mad at me for agreeing to check on you for her. I did it for purely selfish reasons. I don't get to see enough of you regularly."

"Well, once the fool doctor gives me the go-ahead, I'll be driving again and you'll be sick of me."

"Never." Heather held the container out to Aunty Em. "I know you don't need me to cook for you, but I made too much salad for my lunch and thought maybe you could use it."

"That's awful nice of you," the old woman said. "But you know, you shouldn't be fussing over me. You should be finding yourself a man and fussing over him."

Heather just laughed and followed Aunty Em inside. "You're friends with Gloria Waterstone, aren't you? Is she planning on attending the festival this year?"

"I don't know." Aunty Em said and took a casserole out of the oven. "Why?"

"Alex's name has come up as a possible replacement for Owen Philips as a grand marshall this year and I—"

"Alex as a grand marshall?" Aunty Em looked stunned, then dropped the casserole on the table rather loudly. "What kind of crazy fool idea is that?"

"It's not crazy." Heather got glasses out of the cabinet and poured iced tea for both of them. "He's accomplished a lot and deserves the honor just as much as Karin."

Aunty Em brought Heather's salad over to the table and motioned for her to sit down. "Well, you just be careful around him."

Heather was confused. "Careful? Why?"

Aunty Em started dishing up the casserole, plopping spoonfuls on the plates with force. "Because Alex Waterstone is up to no good."

Heather sighed. This wasn't the type of dinner conversation she had hoped for. "He's a well-respected university professor."

"So he says."

"He is," she said. "Penny had him in class."

"One class, that's all he teaches," Aunty Em said. "And Penny says he never dates."

Heather refused to find that piece of information intriguing and started eating. "Maybe he's serious about someone who lives someplace else. He does travel a lot, you know."

"Does he?" Aunty Em was interested. "He have many guests?"

Heather thought about it for a minute. "Actually, no. He rarely has anyone over that I can remember."

"Ha! See, I told you. Up to no good."

"That's no proof. So he doesn't have a lot of friends

in Chesterton. He was gone for years. Maybe his friends just don't come here.''

"Speaking of which, why did he move back here anyway?''

This conversation was getting too bizarre. "Maybe because it had been his home. Lots of people move back home after traveling around a bit.''

Aunty Em just pushed back from the table. "I think he's a spy.''

"A spy!'' Heather just stared at the older woman.

"Yep. He's mysterious, travels a lot and never tells you anything when you ask him a question.''

"That hardly means he's a spy,'' Heather pointed out. "He could just be the type that keeps to himself.''

"I bet if we followed him we'd find him going to dark alleys at midnight in a trench coat.''

Or bright parking lots in daylight? Why had he been in that neighborhood anyway? Heather shook herself. She was not going to get caught up in Aunty Em's fantasies. "Well, we aren't going to follow him so we'll never know for sure. Can I have another helping, please?''

Aunty Em put several large spoonfuls of the casserole on Heather's plate. "I wonder what kind of gun he has.''

Heather froze. No, she had dreamed that. He hadn't had a gun the other night. She had imagined it. "He's a professor,'' she said, but her voice sounded weak and less convinced than before.

Aunty Em gave her a look. "What have you got before school starts again? A week?''

"About that.''

The older woman nodded. "Enough time to do a little investigating. I've got my own PI firm. Well, I will when I finish my correspondence course. We'll get started right away."

An investigation? What in the world was Aunty Em talking about? "I don't think we ought to." Heather stopped. Wouldn't it be best to know if her neighbor was more than a mild-mannered university professor? Finding out would certainly be a brave thing. And didn't she owe it to Dorothy and Toto for all they'd done for her over the years?

Heather took a deep breath and put her fork down. "Okay," she said. "What do we do?"

"Rough evening?" the man said.

Alex turned, hot dog in one hand and a beer in the other. He'd been contemplating the fenced-in parking lot, stewing over this whole mess with Heather as he waited to leave for his meeting with Casio. Next to him stood one of the gambling den's security guards.

Alex forced himself back into his role. "Just a little break in the action. Came out to catch my breath."

"That's a good idea." The man lit up a cigarette and leaned on the fence himself, looking away from Alex. "Sometimes a man needs to step back and get his nerves settled. Just like Michael Jordan when he's about to take a free throw."

Alex nodded and took a bite of the hot dog. "Luck's gonna turn. I can feel it in my bones."

"That's good." The man took a deep drag on his cigarette then crushed it beneath his foot. "Real good." He turned and strode away.

Alex went back to eating his hot dog, though it was sitting pretty heavy in his stomach. All he could see was Heather's vivid eyes this morning, downplaying her asthma. Her delight in rescuing Bonnie and her certainty that love was all that was needed to heal a fearful heart.

She lived in a dreamworld that he had never even visited. Okay, maybe before his father had died, it had been his world, too. But not since. And never would be again either, not that he wanted to go back. No, he was where he belonged right now. He just had to push Heather back where she belonged.

Alex glanced at his watch. It was just about time. Casio had left the shady casino an hour ago, and it should be safe for Alex to leave now, too. He pulled away from the fence, about to take the last bite of his hot dog, when he saw a cat in the parking lot staring at him.

It was a mangy-looking little thing, brown and white in color with green eyes and ragged ears. Most likely mean as all hell—had to be to survive on these streets—and it was staring right at Alex, accusingly.

"Hey, I'm trying," he muttered to the creature. "I know she doesn't belong in this mess. And I'm gonna get her out of it. Just give me a chance."

The cat was still staring at him and Alex looked at the piece of hot dog he still held in his hand, then tossed it to the cat. "Here you go, buddy." Alex said, throwing the hot dog toward the cat.

The cat crept up to the piece of meat, while its eyes darted all around, making sure that danger wouldn't come pouncing on it. Then, after a tentative bat, he snatched up the scrap of hot dog and ran under a car to eat it.

If that cat had been Heather, she would have come over and thanked him for the food, certain that everybody could be trusted. Alex swallowed hard. He was not going to be the one to help her learn that wasn't true.

Alex hustled to the corner and caught the bus about to pull away. After four bus transfers, two train rides, and an hour spent in a shopping mall to lose any possible tails, Alex walked into the hotel suite Casio was using as an office. His supervisor looked about to break a blood vessel.

"What's wrong?" Casio said, almost shouting. "You been made? Something go wrong with the loan?"

Alex flung himself down in a chair across from Casio. "Everything's fine with our caper. I got the loan just fine. First payment is due next week."

"Then—"

Alex fixed Casio with a hard gaze. "I don't want my neighbor involved in this operation."

Casio frowned. "She's not involved."

"I don't want her to be even a bit player."

His supervisor looked away and shook his head. "Don't worry. She's in no danger."

"I want her out." He glared at his supervisor until Casio turned back to look at him. "Totally."

"There something going on between you two?" Casio asked.

Alex laughed. He hoped it sounded better to Casio than it did to him. "Of course not."

"Then what's your problem?"

"My problem is…" That he liked her. That he admired her. "I went to school with the woman. I know her family, her friends."

"She got herself involved by butting in. I can't help that these goons have her pegged as your lady. Besides, I told you," Casio said, "there's no danger to her."

"You can't predict that absolutely for sure," Alex replied. "And I don't want to take a chance."

"Look—" Casio leaned forward on his desk "—we're prepared to—"

"I'm prepared to quit the task force," Alex said quietly.

Casio's mouth opened and shut several times, making him look like a guppy in a fish tank. Alex could feel his stomach churn. He didn't want to leave the task force. He wanted to bring this operation down, but he was not about to put Heather in any danger. And no, not because the two of them had something going. It just wasn't the right thing to do.

"I said we'd protect her," Casio murmured.

"Can you absolutely guarantee that nothing will happen to her?"

"Hell." Casio shook his head. "I can't guarantee that for myself."

"Then she's out," Alex said. "Far out."

Casio leaned back and stared at the ceiling. Time dragged like it wasn't having any fun. Finally, he brought his gaze back on Alex. "Okay."

Chapter Six

Heather heard a noise somewhere deep in her sleep and jerked awake, her heart racing and her blood pounding as she sat up. It was just starting to get light and she was on the sofa in the living room where she must have fallen asleep while watching for Alex to come home.

But Alex coming home wasn't what she heard, it was more like—

The doorbell sounded again, sending Heather flying to her feet. Who would come over at this hour? She peered over at the clock on the mantel; it was just past four. Something must be wrong. She raced to the front door, getting there just as the bell rang again.

She pulled the door open, only to find Aunty Em there, all smiles.

"Aunty Em?" Heather said, gasping for breath. "What are you doing here? Is something wrong?"

"The only thing wrong is that you aren't dressed yet," the older lady snapped. She pushed past Heather and came into the house. "Although I suppose your pajamas are as good a disguise as any. You could claim you were sleepwalking if you're caught."

"Caught doing what?" Heather asked and then frowned. "Why are you here?"

"We got ourselves a job to do." Aunty Em went over to the dining room table and dropped her folder and a small duffel bag. It made a small clunking sound.

Heather could feel her stomach grind and twist. Oh no, it was this crazy investigation Aunty Em had talked about last night. Why had Heather agreed to go along with it? She should have said up front that it was against the law and she was not going to be involved.

"Okay." Aunty Em took some papers out of a folder, spreading them across Heather's breakfast table. "Here's what we're gonna—"

"It's four o'clock in the morning," Heather pointed out. "Alex won't be up yet, if he's even home. I never heard him come in last night."

"Oh yeah?" Aunty Em looked even more interested and hurried over to the dining room window. She pulled back the curtains slightly and peered out. "I don't see a car in his garage."

So he hadn't come home last night. Heather felt her spirits sag even as she told herself she was a fool. She knew he had a life and that she was no part of it. "Well, I guess the investigation will have to wait."

"Why?" Aunty Em hurried back to her papers on the dining room table and shuffled through them. "This is a real stroke of luck, him not being home. I just finished a chapter on lock picking. We can take a look inside now instead of just taking a look around the outside.''

"Inside his house?" Heather asked, her stomach going all quivery. "Wouldn't that be against the law?"

"Oh pishposh," Aunty Em said with a snort and pulled something out of her bag. "It may appear that way but that's only on the surface."

"How is something only against the law on the surface?" Victoria came over to Heather, rubbing against her leg to be picked up. Heather gratefully clutched the warm little body, but it didn't dispel her worries.

"Because it looks like you're doing one thing that might be illegal—that's the surface part—but you're really doing something else. Something good and noble. That's below the surface." She pulled some more things from her bag.

"I don't understand," Heather said.

"That's because you're not a trained investigator like I am." Aunty Em put on a Kiss the Cook apron and tied the strings behind her waist. "Just do what I tell you and don't worry."

Don't worry? Heather was beyond worry, she was ready to hyperventilate. "What if we trigger some kind of alarm? A whole bunch of police cars could come flying out and we could get shot."

"He doesn't have an alarm system. I checked."

"How?"

Aunty Em's frown barely concealed her impatience. "I looked at his front yard. People with alarm systems have to have those little signs stuck in the ground someplace by their door. He doesn't have one."

Heather took a deep breath. She was feeling more and more lightheaded. "I think I'm going to have an asthma attack."

"You're fine," Aunty Em said and put a little packet of tools into one of her apron pockets, a pencil-thin flashlight in another, and a sheaf of papers in a third. "Once we get inside, I'll take the kitchen and you search his bedroom. Then we'll each work our way toward the other."

"What if he comes home while we're inside?"

"Then you vamp him," Aunty Em said.

Heather just stared at the older woman. Did Aunty Em remember who she was talking to? If Heather had any spare air, she would have laughed. "I can't vamp him. I don't know how."

"Every woman knows how to vamp a man. We're born with it. Like being able to bake an apple pie."

"I've never vamped anybody in my whole life," Heather wailed. "I'm getting a rash just thinking about it."

"Look, Heather, stop worrying." Aunty Em's voice was soft and low. Almost soothing. "This is going to be just fine. It's something we have to do. It's our duty. It's for God and country."

For God and country? Heather wasn't even going to question the absurdity of that. "He hasn't done anything wrong, Aunty Em."

"He's got some secret," the older woman said. "I just know it."

"No, he—" The image of Alex stumbling along the dirty streets of Chicago came to Heather's mind. She had been too chicken to ask him what he'd been doing there and he'd never told her, but it certainly wasn't anything to do with Shakespeare's rhyming couplets. Aunty Em was right, he did have a secret.

But secrets didn't have to be the hiding of something bad. They could just be a burden that he was unable to share, or that he had no one to share with. Maybe he needed help but didn't know to ask her.

"Okay," Heather said. "You have an extra flashlight for me?"

Alex pawed at his radio-alarm clock with no success, then suddenly sat straight up in bed. Four twenty-three in the morning? It wasn't his alarm clock buzzing. It was his house alarm.

He grabbed up the security remote from his nightstand and punched in the four digit code. The alarm deactivated, the buzzing stopped, and he could breathe. Now he just had to see what set it off. He entered another code and "bk dr" flashed across the tiny screen. Someone was at his back door. Hopefully, just another kitten.

Slipping his handgun from under the mattress, Alex moved silently from room to room, quickly checking each as he made his way to the kitchen. No sign of anything amiss. Maybe it was just some local kids, not seeing the car parked in the alley instead of the driveway where he usually put it, and thought nobody was home. He doubted it would be any of the gambling crowd. He wasn't due to miss his first loan payment until next week.

He checked the front door, then slipped into the kitchen. The scratching at his back door indicated somebody was out there. Taking a deep breath, Alex crept across the shadowed kitchen.

Through the window in the door, he could see a brightness filling the sky over Heather's garage. It gave him enough light to make out two figures at his door. And enough light to identify them. His lips tightened in irritation.

"Good Lord," he grumbled and looked for a place to put his gun. He couldn't exactly put it in his waistband since he was wearing boxer shorts and nothing else. He stuck the weapon in his silverware drawer, slammed it shut, and jerked opened his back door.

"What the hell are you two doing here?" he growled.

Heather must have jumped ten feet in the air, while Aunty Em dropped what she was holding and faltered back a few steps. He stared at the tool laying on his porch. A lock pick?

"I might ask you the same thing," Aunty Em said, sounding all huffy. "What are you doing, shouting at two ladies?"

But Alex barely heard her, his gaze had moved on to Heather. She looked ready to faint, her face was pale and her eyes wide. But it was the gentle curves beneath the umbrella-carrying cats and dogs on her pajamas that intrigued him. He felt a stirring in his soul, a fire starting to smolder and he grew even more annoyed— but with himself this time. He turned back to Aunty Em.

"What are you doing on my porch? Trying—" he looked pointedly at the lock pick still laying on the ground "—to jimmy my door?"

"Ah…" Aunty Em looked down at the tool, then turned to Heather. "Heather, tell Alex what we're doing here."

"What we're doing here?" Heather half cried.

She looked so bewildered and panic-stricken that Alex wanted to either pick her up and throw her over the back fence into her own yard, or take her in his arms and tell her everything was going to be all right. How was it that both choices involved taking her in his arms? He didn't like what was happening to him. He could not allow it to continue and took a step back.

"Somebody tell me what you two are doing here," he snapped, looking from Heather to Aunty Em. "Anybody."

But neither responded.

"Are we chasing another kitten?" he tried.

"Kitten?" Aunty Em said and turned to frown at Heather.

The young woman almost visibly leapt at the excuse. "Yes, yes." She nodded. "I think it's a littermate to Bonnie."

"Bonnie?" Aunty Em asked, still frowning.

Alex frowned. Heather's fear plucked at some previously unknown strings in his heart. They tugged at him, tried to wear down his resolve, but he'd be damned if he'd let them win. "And the kitten ran into my house," he said.

"It did?" Heather replied.

"Sure, that's why you two were trying to break in."

Heather and Aunty Em looked at each other while Alex shook his head.

This whole thing would have been funny, in a surreal kind of a way, if it wasn't for the danger that Heather was placing herself in. He'd gone through a lot of trouble to get her off his playground and didn't want her stumbling back on it. She was just too damn vulnerable. Anybody within ten miles would see that she was the weak link in the chain. He had to get her out of here and fast.

"I'm sure there's a good reason for these fun and games," he said, trying to sound as snotty and sarcastic as the image he'd developed over the past several months. "But why don't we just forget about it? You guys go back home and, since it's not even four-thirty yet, I'll go back to bed.''

Heather bit at her bottom lip, looking both outrageously innocent and alluring at the same time. He held his breath as if that would keep the warmth flowing from her from getting inside him. It didn't work.

"You're right," Heather said and took a step back as her body seemed to sag in defeat. "We're sorry about—"

"Oh, my knee!" Aunty Em cried and half stumbled as she clutched in the vague direction of her left leg. "Oh, my goodness."

Alex reached out to grab Aunty Em's arm. "What's wrong?"

"Aunty Em," Heather cried at the same time as she rushed to the older woman's other side. "Are you all right? Let's get you home."

Alex tightened his hold of her. "Why don't I—"

"I just need to sit down for a minute," Aunty Em said, and moved her weak, lame body briskly into Alex's kitchen where she plopped down into a kitchen chair. "Oh, that's so much better."

She hadn't needed much help, Alex noted with a frown. It was obvious that the two of them wanted to come inside for some reason and the old lady's bum knee had just been a ruse. Well, at least, they were out of sight from anyone passing by.

But when he glanced over at Heather in those silly pajamas that highlighted her every curve, his breath came harder and his blood raced. The danger level had increased somehow and he needed to go on the attack.

"As long as you're inside, now you can tell me what's going on," he snapped. "Unless Aunty Em's knee is suddenly better and you can go."

"What do you mean, what's going on?" Aunty Em demanded. "You never heard of being neighborly?"

"Neighborly?" Alex repeated.

"Yes," Heather cried in a rush. "We came over to make you breakfast."

"You were breaking into my house to make me breakfast?"

"We weren't breaking in," Aunty Em insisted. "We just wanted it to be a surprise."

"Breakfast is the most important meal of the day, you know," Heather said as she opened his refrigerator.

He turned to look at her and, heaven help him, the sight of her in his kitchen in her pajamas and slippers was almost more than he could bear. He was strong, he was tough. He had stood up to armed felons and never flinched. He had talked desperadoes into releasing hostages. He wasn't going to let one small little wisp of a woman do him in. If they were determined to make him breakfast before they left, he would let them. Maybe this was some sort of a bet.

"I'll have toast," he said and leaned against the kitchen counter.

"Toast?" Heather cried, her hands full of eggs, sticks of margarine and bread. "That's no breakfast. You need something substantial. Something like—"

"Like what he needs," Aunty Em said.

Heather must not have understood either for she just stopped and stared at the older woman. "What he needs?"

Aunty Em was giving Heather some meaningful looks that seemed to make Heather rather nervous all of a sudden. What were they up to now?

"And orange juice with the toast," he added, just to save them the time and trouble of making coffee.

"Okay," Heather said and put the food down on the counter. But her voice was vague and he wasn't sure if she was talking to him or Aunty Em. "Orange juice and toast."

"Can you find the orange juice, honey?" Aunty Em asked her. "Maybe Alex can help you."

He thought the whole purpose of this visit was to make breakfast for him, but he didn't mention that as he moved over to the refrigerator. "It's right over here," he said and pulled the carton from the shelf in the door.

"Oh, thanks," Heather said, her eyes wide and her voice soft.

Soft but packing a mighty wallop. He felt a trembling down to his toes. "Sure, no problem," he said, not about to show any emotion. Not about to feel any—not any more, that is.

From the corner of his eye he caught sight of Aunty Em gesturing impatiently at Heather. He turned once more to frown at Heather who was now a step closer to him.

"Could you get a glass from the cupboard, too?" she asked.

It was a little harder to breathe near her and a little harder to show no reaction, but he could do it. The sooner he finished their little game, the sooner they would leave. It had to be a bet or a dare or some sort of practical joke. He took a glass out of the cabinet over the stove and handed it to her.

Their hands brushed slightly and a flame leapt along his skin, burning a path from her touch to his heart. He had the almost undeniable urge to pull her into his arms. To kiss that worry from her lips and turn that blush into the fire of desire.

He took a hasty step back, back to where sanity reposed. "Anything else?" he asked. But his voice wasn't as brusque and impatient as he would have liked, so he glanced at the clock on the stove. "I hate to rush you all, but I've got to be going soon."

"Where does a college professor go at 5:00 a.m.?" Aunty Em wanted to know.

Anywhere where he could breathe and think and be in control. "A meeting," was all he said though.

"We're bothering you then, aren't we?" Heather asked as she got bread out of the package and slipped it into the toaster.

Bothering him? "No, of course not," he lied. "I was getting up soon anyway and it's nice to have the company."

"It's awful early for an ordinary meeting," Aunty Em pointed out.

"Ah, but I don't have ordinary meetings," he said. "As an extraordinary professor, I have extraordinary meetings."

Aunty Em frowned at him. Or was it at Heather?

"I wish I could take one of your classes," Heather said—how had she gotten so close again? "Do you ever teach in the evening?"

"Not usually," he said. Retreating back another step would be a sign of weakness—but maybe wisdom too. Except he was already backed up against the refrigerator.

"What a shame," Heather said.

Damn, but she had the most beautiful blue eyes. As wide as the sky, with as much promise and mystery too.

"So who's your next target?" Aunty Em asked.

Heather blinked and those marvelous eyes disappeared for a split second, long enough to break the spell and for Aunty Em's words to penetrate. "Huh?"

"We know that you're not just a professor."

Alex turned to look at her, icy fingers of fear climbing up and down his back. They knew? All that work so many people had gone through to establish his cover and now, in the flick of an eyelash, he found out it was for naught. How in the world had his cover been blown?

"So what foreign power are you working for?"

"Foreign power?"

"It's okay, Alex," Heather told him. She took his hand in hers and he felt a searing heat wash over him. "You probably got into it accidentally."

Got into what? He might be following this conversation better if Heather was fully dressed and not holding his hand, but he doubted it.

"Don't make excuses for him, girl," Aunty Em snapped, then glared at Alex once more. "So who are you working for?"

Alex didn't know what the hell was going on but, fortunately, it didn't seem that Aunty Em or Heather did either. He slipped his hand from Heather's and took a step around her to pour himself a glass of orange juice just as the toast popped up.

"Who am I working for?" he repeated as Heather turned. "I'm afraid—"

Out of the corner of her eye, he saw Heather pull open the silverware drawer. And before he could react, her face turned white as a bedsheet, she let out a blood-curdling scream and then crumpled.

Alex caught her before she hit the floor, managing to close the silverware drawer at the same time.

Heather felt a cold, icy weight on her forehead and a cold wet nose on her cheek. Unfortunately, she knew what both things were—an ice pack because she had fainted and Henry seeing if she was okay. Just her luck, no amnesia.

"Oh, good, you're awake," Aunty Em said. "Alex wanted to call an ambulance, but I told him you'd be fine. Glad to see you didn't prove me a liar."

Heather tried to sit up, glancing around the room with a franticness that she hoped wasn't obvious. Henry was on the bed with her, Victoria was on the dresser watching and Aunty Em was on a chair pulled up to the bedside. No one else was visible.

"How did I get here?" she asked.

"Alex carried you," Aunty Em said. "You had him really worried, too. Have to say his concern surprised me. Maybe I misjudged the man."

No, you didn't, Heather wanted to say, but she couldn't make the words come out. "Where is he now?" she asked instead.

"Oh, I sent him home. No use having him underfoot when we're trying to chat." The older woman leaned in closer. "So what made you scream and faint?"

Aunty Em was staring at her expectantly and suddenly Heather knew she couldn't tell her. Not about the gun. Not about the fact that Alex had to be hiding something. And certainly not about the way her heart raced at the mere thought of him.

"I saw a bug," Heather said and looked away. She dared just a quick glance back at Aunty Em, who was frowning, and then reached over to pet Henry. "I know it was silly but it was a big bug and it scared me. I guess maybe I was lightheaded since I hadn't eaten any breakfast.''

"Why didn't you say you needed to eat before we went?"

"I don't know. I didn't think about it." She wasn't crazy about this line of conversation. "What time is it anyway? Was I out for long?"

"It's not even six. Plenty of time for you—"

"But what about you?" Heather rushed on. "Don't you have to write up the day's schedule for the tree trimming crews at the tree farm?"

The older woman's frown deepened and she looked again at the clock by the side of Heather's bed. "You're right," she said with a sigh. "Penny left me in charge when she went to Paris. I'd better go."

"Are you sure you can drive home okay?" Heather asked.

"I'm more concerned about leaving you alone," Aunty Em said as she got to her feet. "You still look as pale as a ghost. Maybe I ought to call—"

"No," Heather cried before Alex's name could even be mentioned. "I'm fine. Really."

Though Aunty Em looked far from convinced, she did leave and Heather settled back down on the bed. Victoria snuggled up on one side of her and Henry on the other. Neither of them seemed to care that she'd made such a fool of herself. Heather only wished she could be as blasé.

"I just didn't want Aunty Em to be right," she told them. "I didn't want Alex to be a spy or a bank robber or anything bad."

It was crazy. It didn't make any sense. But she

wanted to pretend that Alex was just a college professor. Victoria cuddled up even closer to Heather.

"Heather?"

Alex! Heather's heart practically stopped as she sat back up. Her mouth went dry as a desert and her head felt even more wobbly than before. It sounded like he was in her kitchen. What could he want?

Victoria and Henry dove under the bed and Heather fought the temptation to join them. It wouldn't be ladylike and not at all polite. But she just couldn't face him—not after the fool she'd made of herself this morning. If she couldn't hide under the bed, there was always the closet or the bathroom. Ignoring her spinning head, she scrambled off her bed and into the bathroom, silently closing the door just as she heard his footsteps outside her bedroom.

"Heather? I'd really like to talk to you."

She leaned back against the closed door. His voice was so deep and did the craziest things to her stomach. It made her nervous, but not exactly out of fear. It did make her long for things that she only dreamed vaguely about, and that was reason enough to steer clear of him!

"I was just going to take a shower," she called out. She ought to turn the water on to make it sound realistic, but the effort was too much for her. She let her fingers clutch at the towel hanging on the back of the door.

"Could we talk first?" he asked.

He was so close. In her room now, she knew. She should open the door and come out. She should smile at him and tell him everything was fine. Make some little joke about the gun and her fainting, and then offer to finish making him breakfast.

Right. She could do all that as well as she could vamp. Her face flushed with the sudden memory of her idiocy. Vamping indeed! She could never ever face him again.

"I really haven't got time," she called out to him. "I have a teacher's workshop today."

"It's just barely six."

"It's in South Bend." That was an hour's drive. Surely plausible.

He said nothing for a moment but she knew he was still there. She couldn't exactly hear him breathing, but she could feel it. What was the matter with her? Maybe she was still dizzy. She tried to let the coolness of the ceramic tile floor ooze up into her.

"I just wanted to make sure you were all right," he finally said.

She was hot all over again. After they had broken into his house, he was checking to make sure she was fine? How could someone that nice be a spy?

"I'm fine," Heather called out and stared at the jar of seashell-shaped soap that she had gotten from one of her students. She took a slow steadying breath and told herself she could do this. She was an expert at getting out of scary situations.

"I faint all the time when I see bugs," she yelled through the door. "It's no big deal."

"Bugs?" He sounded surprised.

She bit at her lip and wrapped her shaking arms around her body. "Yeah, it was a huge one," she told him. "It ran across my foot."

"A bug?" he repeated. "You fainted because you saw a bug?"

"Silly, isn't it? But that's me."

"I thought maybe you had—"

"Summer's really a bad time for me." She didn't want to know what he was going to say. "Bugs all over the place and I'm fainting right and left. Nobody invites me to barbecues anymore."

"I guess not."

His voice was thoughtful, uncertain. She closed her eyes in relief and managed to move a step or two, enough to sink onto the edge of the bathtub. He was buying it.

"Thanks for checking up on me," she called out. "But I'm fine. Don't have time to be anything but fine with the festival coming up so soon."

He didn't say anything and a little wave of panic washed over her. Maybe he wasn't buying it. Maybe he was suspicious, or annoyed. Or even worried that she was trying to latch onto him.

"I have so many Oz costumes to finish," she said quickly. "I bet we won't even see each other for the next month." Was that long enough? "Or maybe even a couple of months. Maybe we should wish each other a Merry Christmas now, just in case."

"Yeah, maybe," he said.

It had to be her imagination, but his voice sounded odd. Not quite disappointed which would make no sense. Resigned maybe. No, it was the echoes in the room, that was all.

"So Merry Christmas," she said.

"Uh, Happy New Year."

There was no mistaking the odd tone this time, but she didn't try to read any meaning into it. Holding her breath, she waited. After a moment that lasted several centuries, she heard him leave the room and a minute later she heard her back door close.

She let her breath out with a sigh and leaned against

the bathroom wall. Alex Waterstone was a spy. A bad guy. If this was a movie, he'd be wearing a black hat and everyone would boo when he came on the screen. If this was Oz, he'd be the Wicked Wizard of the West.

Now she knew one way to win that bet with Toto— get proof of Alex's evilness and turn him in. But she could never do that.

Chapter Seven

Alex walked out to the street with the student tutors, keeping his eyes from straying over to Heather's house. He refused to find interest in the fact that lights were still on in her living room, so she must still be awake. He would not wonder what was keeping her up until midnight tonight when her lights were normally out by ten. And he certainly would not give a moment's thought to the question of which pajamas she was wearing tonight—the cats or the teddy bears.

It should be getting easier to ignore Heather; it'd been a week since he'd spoken to her. A week of long hours spent undercover. A week of coming home for short breaks at odd hours. A week of holding his breath with worry and anticipation every time the doorbell sounded or the phone rang thinking it could be Heather.

A week of being so on edge that his relief felt almost

like disappointment when it wasn't her at the door. Which was crazy, because this was what he wanted. This was what he had to do to keep her safe. And right now, he had to be concentrating on the undercover work and the fact that, as planned, he had missed his first loan payment. He didn't need any distractions. Not his next-door neighbor, not her cats, not anything.

This meeting this evening with his student tutors had helped remind him that his real job was to catch some crooks.

"With the Labor Day weekend here, be flexible with your schedules. We aren't jailers," Alex said as the students stopped near their cars. "Any last questions?"

"Yeah. Can we get extra tickets to the home opener?" one of the students asked him. "My brother's coming in and I'd like him to see the game."

Alex laughed. "I'll see what I can do. At least you gave me a week to figure something out."

"If you can get him another ticket, I might have a brother coming too," another student said.

They all laughed and then piled into the cars parked along the street in front of Alex's home. After much waving, honking and revving of engines, they pulled away from his house. They turned at the light two blocks down and disappeared from sight. The quiet of the night returned and the darkness got even thicker. The streetlights seemed unable to penetrate the shadows. It reminded him of the night Heather had come into his yard to catch Bonnie.

He turned toward her house. He hadn't wanted to but his head did. How was the little cat doing? Had she progressed enough to be let out of the cage, or maybe even out of the room? Just one more thing he would never know. One more thing that it was best he didn't know.

He turned to go back to his own house and saw something light-colored down by the sidewalk at the other side of her yard. It looked like a paper. Well, that was one thing he could do for her, pick up some stray trash from her yard.

He went over and plucked the page from a free advertising newspaper from her lawn, crumpling it in his hand as he took a close look at her house. The bushes were a little high by that window, but otherwise the place looked pretty secure. Though that evergreen to the right of her door should really be trimmed back. And that sprinkler hose should definitely be—

"Yo, professor."

Alex turned, taken by surprise. "Did you leave something here?"

But it wasn't one of his students. It was a large man in slacks and a suit coat who was now only a step or two away. A second man, shorter but just as wide, wasn't far behind. Only then did Alex notice the dark sedan parked farther down the street.

Damn. The loan shark's collection squad. Where had his mind been? Life in Chesterton was making him careless.

"We didn't leave nothing, but a little bird said you was supposed to," the large man said as he pushed Alex. A mixture of sweat, testosterone, and beer filled the air around him.

"Hey," Alex said and started forward only to stop. He was a professor. A wimpy, untrained professor who not only couldn't fight back, but wouldn't. Damn, Chesterton was fogging his mind.

He let his shoulders droop and darted quick glances

at the men. "I just need a little more time," he said, whining the practiced lines even as he heard a noise behind him, a sound like a window opening in Heather's house.

Damn. He closed his eyes in brief anguish. That was all he needed after working so hard to keep her uninvolved. He had to get this over with quickly and quietly. Or at least, move it away from Heather's front yard.

He smiled at the thugs, hoping they could see his grin in the shadowy night. Hoping they would let him move over ten or twenty feet. "If you come—"

But they weren't about to let him do anything. "How about you come up with the money you owe?" the second thug muttered, his lips clamped around his cigarette. He grabbed for Alex's shirtfront.

Only at the same time, Alex had been taking a step toward his yard and away from Heather's. The man's sudden movement caused Alex to automatically move sideways, tangling his foot in Heather's garden hose. He tottered for a moment, trying to regain his balance, and failed. He fell backward as if he'd been tackled and hit the base of his skull on something hard and unmoving. The garden sprinkler, he thought briefly as darkness threatened to claim him.

"What the hell did you have to hit him for?" the bigger man whispered sharply to his partner. "We were just supposed to push him around a little."

"I didn't hit him," the second man murmured back. "I just pushed him a little and he fell. He must have a glass head."

Alex fought back the dizziness. He started to sit up but stopped. Maybe it would be better for them to think they'd knocked him out. Maybe then they'd leave and

Heather would have nothing else to hear and come investigate.

Alex closed his eyes, willing the thugs to leave. Unfortunately, he had fallen into a bed of flowers and the sweet smell was overpowering. He felt a sneeze coming on. Why couldn't Heather have a plain old lawn instead of flower beds at every corner?

One of the men nudged Alex with his foot and Alex moaned softly for effect. He was down, they could leave. So why weren't they?

"What do we do with him?" the first man whispered.

"The streetlights ain't very bright. Let's just leave him here."

Yes, Alex agreed silently. Leave me here and go.

"Better we should put him inside his house."

That would be okay too, Alex thought. Take him inside where innocent strangers wouldn't get involved.

"Uh, I dunno. Looks like somebody's moving around inside."

What were they talking about? There was no one in his house. Damn. The fog in his brain parted for a split second. They thought Heather's house was his!

"How about we dump him on the porch?"

"Great. Grab his feet. I'll take his shoulders."

"No." Alex rolled away from them and got to his feet. The world wobbled a bit, but nothing major. Nothing he couldn't handle. "I'm okay."

The smaller man laughed and tossed his cigarette to the side. "Looks like the doc is afraid of the old lady."

Alex frowned, a slow anger starting to simmer. He wasn't afraid of anything, certainly not Heather. But he didn't like this jerk talking about her. He didn't like the fact that they knew Heather was even around.

"How could anyone be afraid of someone in those dumb pajamas?" the other man said.

The two thugs had been looking in Heather's windows! Alex's anger was slow no more. It exploded sky-high. These jerks were not allowed to laugh at Heather. She was sweet and gentle and caring. He grabbed the nearer thug, pulling him up by his shirtfront.

"Leave her alone, you little worm," Alex snapped.

"Hey, doc!" the other man snarled.

"Hello? Is someone out there?" Heather called from the house.

Alex turned, his heart stopping. She wasn't coming outside, was she? Then something solid connected with his chin, blackness swallowed him and he was falling backward. Away from the sprinkler, he hoped.

He felt a solid thunk on the back of his head, and had a brief realization that his hopes weren't to be answered before everything really went black this time.

Heather stepped out onto the front porch. Good. Alex's company was gone and she could move her sprinkler. She hadn't been about to run outside in her pajamas while he and his friends had been out in front. Not that any of them would notice or care what she was wearing.

She crept out onto the lawn, hoping no one was looking out their windows. Or that no bats were flying around low. Billy Mason told her class this morning that one had gotten into his house last week.

She stopped, horror freezing her mind as she saw something on the yard near the sidewalk. What if it was a raccoon? No, it was too big for that. A bear, maybe? Did they even have bears around here? She didn't think so and, swallowing hard, inched closer. The lump on the ground moved slightly.

Heavens, it was Alex!

The wobbliness of his movements as he tried to sit up pushed everything else from Heather's thoughts and she raced over to his side.

"Alex? Are you all right? What happened?" She knelt down on the dew-damp grass.

He was frowning at her as if he didn't know who she was. Gracious, had he been mugged again? But no one ever got mugged in Chesterton!

"Are those the cats or the teddy bears?" he asked.

Oh, no. He was delirious. This was serious. She wrestled for a moment with her conscience, then knew what she had to do.

She reached over and slipped his arm around her shoulders. The closeness did funny things to her breathing and to her heart, but she promised herself she would not pay attention to such nonsense. This wasn't the time to get all silly.

"Let's get you inside," she told him. "We can talk about it then."

She put her arm around his waist. Golly, it was solid. He must be all muscle. She wondered if his arms were as strong. He could probably lift her with one hand. What would it be like to dance with him?

A raindrop landed on her arm, then another and another. A timely reminder to get her mind back where it belonged and stop dragging out all sorts of foolish fantasies.

"I don't need help," he mumbled.

"Of course, you don't." Heather got him slowly to his feet. He was able to stand, but kept rubbing the back of his head.

"Damn but you have a hard sprinkler," he muttered.

"Yes, I'm sorry about that," she murmured. "I keep meaning to get a softer one."

She wasn't sure if he realized that his other arm was around her shoulders, but she wasn't going to point it out. She moved slowly toward her front door, bringing him along like a reluctant horse. Just keep moving, she whispered in her heart. If he fell, she'd have no way to get him inside. Just a few more steps.

But when they reached the spill of light thrown across the grass by the open door, he stopped. "I need to go home," he said.

"You need to get your head looked at," she said. "You could have a concussion or worse."

He took his arm from her shoulders and moved a step away from her. "I'm fine."

"You aren't fine," she informed him. "You got knocked out."

"I just tripped."

Why was he being so stupidly stubborn? "I need to get you to the emergency room."

"I'm not going anywhere."

His voice had taken a definite sharp turn, but she didn't care.

"Then I'll call the paramedics."

"I don't need the paramedics. I'm going home."

"And collapse and die there by yourself," she snapped. "I don't think so, Mr. Know-It-All."

He stopped and stared at her. As well he might. She wasn't sure what had gotten into her, but she was not going to lose this battle.

"I'm not going to die," he told her, but his voice had gotten gentler.

And that gentler tone did something strange to her

heart. It made her bravado double and triple in size. And made her take his hand in hers.

"Come inside and let me look at your head," she said. "If you don't, I'm calling the paramedics and I'll tell them you're acting irrationally."

He sighed, a sound of obvious annoyance and exasperation, but he did come up onto the porch and into the house.

"This really isn't necessary," he pointed out.

"You're irrational, remember?" she said. "You aren't able to judge what's necessary and what isn't. Get in the kitchen. The light is best in there."

She led him into the kitchen, accompanied by Victoria and Henry, and pulled out a chair at the table. The cats bravely sniffed at Alex's feet while she got her flashlight from the pantry. There was purring in the air by the time she turned back, but was it her or her cats?

She didn't have time for such thoughts right now. She grabbed the flashlight and went up behind Alex.

"This really is ridiculous," he said. His grumps had returned.

"Lower your head, please."

She shone the flashlight on the back of his head, suddenly reluctant to run her fingers through his hair. It just seemed so...so...so intimate. But she didn't need to touch him to see the lump at the back of his head.

"Gracious," she cried. "You really took a wallop. What happened?"

"Nothing," he said and got unsteadily to his feet. "I tripped."

This was a man that did every daredevil stunt ever conceived as a kid—and had never gotten hurt. And now she was supposed to believe he had turned clumsy and tripped over her sprinkler? She wasn't that naive. But she wasn't going to pursue the matter just now.

"You need to get that looked at," she said. "I bet you've got a concussion."

He flexed his shoulders. "It wouldn't be the first time. I'll be fine."

He started toward the door, but she was faster and blocked his way. Hands crossed over her chest, she gave him a look that hopefully didn't reveal the way her knees were knocking. Henry darted behind her as backup.

"If you aren't going to the emergency room, you aren't going anywhere," she said. "You need to have someone check on you often. Like every two or three hours."

He was not happy. In fact, he looked pretty darn murderous, but she refused to budge. She knew in a minute, she would collapse. If he said "Boo!" to her, she'd give in. She always had in the past and was certain this would be no different.

But he didn't say "Boo!" or anything else. He just sank back into the chair with a frown. "You don't understand," he said. "I shouldn't be here at all. It'll give everyone the wrong impression."

She laughed at that. If that wasn't the sweetest, most old-fashioned idea. "No one's watching," she assured him. "And if they are, no one cares. Come on, I'll show you the spare room."

Toto slowed his car to a stop and frowned as he peered through the gentle rain at Heather's house. The place was all lit up.

"That's odd," he told Junior. "She's never up this late. We'd better check things out."

Toto turned off the engine, then he and Junior got out. He wasn't sure if the retired police dog liked the rain, but Toto thought it felt good, cooling after the day's heat. Maybe once they got home, they'd take a nice long walk in it. Nothing much to stay at home for anymore. Not since Dorothy had left town.

Penny and Brad were back from Paris. He hadn't actually seen them because seeking them out would look too much like he was anxious for news of Dorothy. Of course, he was, but no one needed to know that.

Toto walked across the lawn, checking out the perimeter of the house. Drapes were closed in most of the windows except in the kitchen where the lights were off. In the light filtering in from the living room he could see one of Heather's cats sitting on top of the refrigerator. It looked pretty calm, just giving itself a bath, so everything was probably all right.

Still, he and Junior climbed the back stairs and pushed open the kitchen door. "Heather?" Toto called softly.

The cat jumped off the refrigerator and disappeared. A moment later, Heather came into the kitchen.

"Toto?"

"What's up?" he asked. She seemed tense.

But Heather just glanced over her shoulder, then pulled Toto back outside. "Nothing's up," she whispered. "Alex is here."

"He is? What for?" This was a strange time of night to drop in on a neighbor. "Is something wrong?"

"Wrong?" Heather seemed flustered. "Why do you ask that?"

"You aren't usually up this late and Alex isn't usually here."

He felt something in the air and saw her lips twist slightly in the pale light coming from the house. Then she smiled.

"Actually, if you must know it's kind of personal."

Toto had never heard a voice blush before, but Heather's did.

"I was cutting out construction paper leaves for my class and he came over to help," Heather continued. "And then we just uh…um…well, you know."

Now it was Toto's turn to blush and he stepped back, farther from the house as if it could ease his embarrassment. "Gosh, Heather, I'm sure sorry. Geez, I didn't mean to interrupt." He shook his head, hoping their stupid dare wasn't at the bottom of all this. But he didn't feel he could ask her. "I'd better go."

"It's fine, really. Thanks for checking."

She put her hand on his arm. Her touch felt cold, almost as if she were afraid or worried. But her voice didn't sound that way. And her cat hadn't acted as if anything was wrong—not until Toto had come in. He took another step back.

"If he's going to be here a while," he suggested, fighting back his chagrin, "maybe he should close his front door."

"It's open?" Heather took a step toward Alex's house, then stopped. "Uh, Toto? Could I borrow Junior overnight? I'm…uh…socializing a new kitten and I'd like to see her with a dog."

Toto looked down at his buddy, the only one who was sticking by him these days. The dog was aquiver with excitement as if he'd understood Heather's request. Tail trembling, mouth panting, his eyes were pleading with Toto.

Toto sighed. "Sure. Why not?"

He could take his walk in the rain by himself. No big deal. So what if everybody in town now had somebody but him. No big deal.

"Will overnight be enough?" he asked. "Junior'll be happy to stay a couple of days and take care of your kitten."

"You don't need him over the Labor Day weekend?" Heather asked.

Toto shook his head. "Actually, it'd be better if he stays with you. I've got to work extra shifts so this way he won't be alone."

"That's great. We'll have a good time, won't we, Junior?"

The big dog wagged his tail. Toto just gave them both a tight smile. It was all right; he was used to being alone. "I'll close up Alex's place, then I'll go on home."

"That's okay," Heather said. "I...ah...I need to get something."

"Now you just stick with me," Heather whispered to Junior as she pulled open Alex's screen door. She heard no sounds from inside so maybe no one was there. Hopefully whoever had mugged Alex had moved on. She took a step inside and Junior rushed past her.

"Junior!" she whispered.

The dog stopped and trotted back to her, but there were no sounds from the rest of the house. She came all the way inside and let the screen door swing shut.

She was in a regular old living room. A sofa and chairs, a TV and some bookshelves.

"I guess we should get his toothbrush," she told Junior.

It sounded perfectly reasonable, but her feet did not want to move. She just stood in the doorway, staring into the rest of the house. A light was on in the kitchen, but the other rooms were dark. Dark and mugger-filled perhaps. Junior didn't move either, and finally she sighed.

"Well, all right. I'll go get it."

She strode briskly across the living room and into the short hallway. With a quickened step, she went into the bathroom and flicked the light on.

She plucked a red toothbrush out of the toothbrush holder, and hurried back out.

"I've got it," she told Junior who didn't look impressed.

"Yes, I know. I'm being silly. But now we can—"

The shrill ringing of the phone split the silence and she froze. Surely her heart stopped beating altogether. No, it was racing. Who would be calling at this hour of the night?

"How silly," she said to Junior. "Just because I don't get calls at this hour, it doesn't mean that Alex can't. Should I answer, do you think?"

But before she could make a decision, Alex's answering machine kicked in. She could hear his voice in the kitchen. Though it was the height of rudeness, she supposed she ought to listen to the caller and relay the message to Alex. It might be important.

She started toward the kitchen, but she didn't need to go there. The caller's voice was loud enough to be heard all over the house.

"Waterstone?" The caller paused to cough. "Things got out of hand tonight so I'm gonna show you what a great guy I am. I'm giving you an extra day to come up with the vigorish. But not a minute more. You come up with the dough by 8:00 p.m. tomorrow or you're liable to be playing tag with some Lake Michigan carp." Another cough. "If you can't handle the pressure, baby, stick to the lottery and leave the big games for the men."

The caller hung up and the dial tone rang out across the room for a long moment. Then there was silence. Deadly silence. Heather looked slowly around the room as if searching for something to prove her awful suspicions false. But she found nothing. No neon signs proclaiming Alex's innocence. No ministers giving testimonials as to the golden quality of his character. Nothing.

Just the awful realization that Alex was a gambler, a bad one apparently. That's surely what he had been doing in Chicago that day he'd been mugged, and this episode tonight was somehow part of it, too. It sounded as if he owed someone a great deal of money, and they would do anything to get it back. He was in terrible trouble.

"Heather?"

She spun around and found Alex standing in his doorway. Had he heard? Did he know that she knew? She had no idea what to say to him. *Stop gambling, why don't you? It's too risky.* Yeah, right. She took a deep breath. No, the best thing was to distract him so he wouldn't ask her anything. But how?

Only one way came to mind.

Chapter Eight

"What are you doing here?" Alex asked.

Okay, maybe his voice was a bit snappish, but Heather had disappeared without a word. He'd gone into the bathroom to wash the lump on the back of his head—figuring that was the only way he could keep Heather from scrubbing it down herself—and when he'd come out she was gone. He'd been certain those thugs had come back. But here she was, walking around in his house with no protection but Junior, as if there weren't dangers all around.

"I'm not doing anything here," Heather told him. "I was coming right back."

But anything could happen in a moment. Anywhere. "Is someone else here?" he asked. "I thought I heard voices."

"No one but me and Junior." She looked guilty, but

she held out his toothbrush. "I just came by to close your doors and get this," she said. Then she smiled.

He had been at the receiving end of smiles before. Smiles that rode lips much more experienced than Heather's. But none packed the same punch. He felt like a boat whose moorings had just been severed. A kite whose string had broken. He suddenly felt cast adrift and his only safety, his very sanity was in her smile.

"I like all the men who stay overnight with me to have their own toothbrush," she said.

It was an outrageous statement, considering their situation. And one that even her voice said was a lie, but still it ignited something in the pit of his stomach. Something that he might have said was jealousy, except that that made no sense at all.

He had to protect her. And the only way to keep her safe was to keep her near him for the time being. Her safety was all he wanted. And the first step was to get her out of his house. Then he needed to move her before anyone made a connection between the two of them.

"You should have just told me that my door was open," he said. "I would have come over and closed it. You shouldn't be wandering around at night."

"I had Junior with me," she pointed out.

"He's—" Alex frowned. "Wait a minute. Where did he come from? He wasn't in your house before."

"Toto stopped by and let me borrow him, but don't worry, I didn't tell him anything."

Her voice was smooth as silk. Her tone told him to relax. Yet the fact that she had taken a few steps closer was all he could think of.

"Anything about what?" he asked.

"About your getting hurt."

But he barely heard her words. There was something in her eyes that he had never seen before—a concern that reached deeper than just the moment. A steadiness that said she could be trusted. A sense of caring that made it hard for him to breathe.

Whatever it was, however she did it, something woke deep in his heart. A strange and lonely yearning, a longing that he had never felt before, an overpowering need to hold on to this moment.

Hell, this was the last thing he needed right now. He had a job to do, a job he wanted to do. A job that had nothing to do with her, except that she had gotten caught up in the fringes. Every instinct as a man told him to run and stay clear of Heather's blue eyes, but at the same time, every instinct as a man also said he had to stay and protect her. There was a rough world outside his door, full of bad men.

"Let's go on back to my place," Heather said, her voice soft as she glided over to his side.

How could someone in teddy bear pajamas glide? But he shook himself free of the trance he'd been falling into. Protect her he would, and that included from himself.

"Sure, I'll just get the lights here." He needed to move away from her, to find a spot where he could think and breathe.

"I'll get the kitchen lights," she offered.

She started across the room. One step away, then two, then three. But breathing didn't come much easier. He turned, hurrying over to the light on the end table. He could manage this, though. It was nothing compared to being shot three times and surviving. Or getting through that night of surveillance in a swamp where mosquitoes were the least of his worries. Or even the time he'd had to steer that burning car away from the crowd of people—and get out himself before it exploded. Staying sane around Heather would be a cinch.

He turned off the light on the far end table at the same time as the lights in the kitchen went out. The room went darker than night, the light filtering in from outside didn't seem to make much difference. He stepped around the low table in front of the sofa.

"Oops," Heather said from somewhere over near the TV. "No, Junior, down. I'm fine."

What was he thinking of? "I'm sorry. I didn't expect it to be so dark. I'll just—"

He turned back toward the light but found Junior in his way. And then when he tried to get around the dog, he found Heather. Somehow they'd walked right into each other's arms. His hands slid around her back, her softness was pressed up against him.

"Oh, my!" she said.

"Sorry," he said.

But was he? And if he was, why couldn't he let go of her?

Her delicate sweet scent surrounded him, pulling him deeper under her spell. His legs would not—could not—move, but his arms just tightened around her, bringing her in closer and closer. His hands found fire wherever he touched.

His head bent and found her lips. Soft, gentle, yet holding so much power. How had he never felt the singe of her fire before? Anywhere near her and he felt scorched with the heat. But touching her, kissing her, tasting her passion, only made his need to hold her stronger. Only made his fire hotter and hungrier.

His lips grew more insistent, speaking their needs through his touch. His arms pulled tighter, his mouth moved more roughly on hers. But it wasn't enough. He couldn't hold her close enough. He couldn't taste her deeply enough. He couldn't answer the screaming need in his heart.

But then Junior barked. A sharp warning bark from over near the door, and it brought Alex back to his senses. He let go of Heather, thanking the stars for the darkness to cover the confusion that must surely be on his face. He turned gratefully to the dog.

"What is it, Junior?"

Alex's eyes had grown accustomed to the dark now and he hurried over to the door. What kind of a man was he that forgot his responsibilities when a beautiful woman was near? He should have been watching, not Junior. But it was just a neighbor walking a dog across the street.

Alex took a deep breath as he felt Heather come up behind him. He was not going to fall again. He would stay alert, stay watchful and Heather would stay safe.

"You ready to go?" he asked. He felt his heart wavering at her nearness. He would need a distraction at her house. "I think I'll just grab a book or two. And some videos."

"But it's late," she pointed out. "Past midnight and that's past my bedtime."

Her words came out on a breathless cloud of sweetness that teased at his senses. But bedtime? There was no way he was getting into a bed in her house.

"It's still early for me," he said as he grabbed up a couple of books off the nearest shelf, and took a couple of videos, too. He couldn't see enough to read the titles, but it hardly mattered. "But don't feel you have to keep me company. In fact, you can sleep even better knowing that me and Junior are on watch duty."

"But your head…"

"It's fine," he assured her as he ushered them out the door. Junior bounded out into the velvety blackness, then Alex pulled the door shut and activated the alarm. Lucky thing the alarm had still been turned off from when the students had come over or Casio—

Damn. Casio. He was probably ready to send out the troops again. Alex should have checked in ages ago. He would call Casio from her house once she was asleep.

They went back into her house where her cats were waiting. Two were greeting Junior like a long-lost buddy, while the little gray one stood across the room hissing.

"Is that Bonnie?" he asked. "She's out of prison?"

"It wasn't prison," Heather argued.

Alex laughed as he went over to pet the little thing. "Yeah, I know. It was for her own good. It was the only way to save her. Sometimes you have to be tough to be kind."

Heather gave him a strange look as she stood up. "Yes, you're right. Sometimes you do."

"Well, I'm going to read for a little bit before I turn in," he said.

"All right." She gave him an odd look as she took a step backward down the hall. "The bed in the spare bedroom is made. I'll get up every few hours to check on you."

"Right." He didn't bother to start the argument that it wasn't necessary. He did have a hell of a headache, but he wasn't going to mention that, either.

She nodded and turned to go down to her room.

Alex, still holding his books and videos, went into the living room. Junior and the cats followed him. When he sank onto the sofa with a sigh, the animals all grouped in front, watching him.

"What?" he whispered at them. "I'm not the bad guy here. You don't have to be suspicious of me. I'm just trying to keep her safe."

He heard the water running in her bathroom, so he got up and quickly checked the front door. It was locked. He checked the two front windows. They were locked, too.

"Alex?"

Hell, she was on her way back. He sped over to the sofa, grabbing up a book as he flopped down. Junior stood by his side, wagging his tail as if this were a new game, while the cats watched warily.

"Alex?" Heather was at the doorway.

He looked up from his contemplation of the table of contents of his book. Her face was a rosy pink, her golden hair a soft halo around her face. She took his breath away.

"There's pop in the refrigerator and cookies in the cabinet."

He smiled. "Thanks. I'm fine, though."

"Okay." She hesitated a moment, then stepped back. "Good night."

"Good night and thanks."

"No problem." But she was already starting down the hall.

He sighed as he heard soft noises from her bedroom, then it was quiet. One of the cats, the calico, had left with Heather. The brown tabby was sitting next to Junior, watching him. Bonnie, the kitten, was maintaining surveillance from under a rocker near the kitchen door. He didn't know if they were expecting entertainment or waiting for him to commit a crime they could report.

"So do you think it's safe to check the windows now?" he whispered.

No one answered or even blinked so he got up and went over to the dining area. The two windows were locked, but he checked the kitchen, the strays' room and the main bath.

He paused at Heather's door, but knew it was too soon to check her windows, and went back to the living room and his book. A dissertation on the use of trees in medieval poetry. He read page one three times and then put the book down.

"How fast does she fall asleep?" he asked the brown cat and got a suspicious frown in answer.

It was almost a half hour since she'd gone to bed. That was long enough, wasn't it? He got to his feet and crept down the hall, pausing just outside her door to listen. At first he heard nothing, then the soft even sounds of her breathing.

He started into the room, only to all but trip over the brown cat racing in ahead of him. The cat jumped on the bed, nearly giving Alex heart failure as he was certain Heather would awaken. But she didn't.

By the soft glow of a night-light, Alex could see the brown cat cuddle up close to her chest with what sure looked like a smirk. Alex just gave the cat a glare and tiptoed over to the far window. He checked to make sure it was locked, then turned back.

In the gentle light, he could see Heather on the bed. She was lying on her side, the curve of her hips tantalizing. His hands itched to run down her side, to feel those curves beneath his touch. His breath came hard and sharp, as the need to feel Heather lying beneath him was almost stronger than he could bear.

He'd felt desire before, but never like this. Never so strong that he could practically smell his flesh burning. Never so strong that he thought his heart would burst. It was as if Heather had cast a spell on him.

She stirred slightly and his breath caught. What was he doing, watching her like this? He sped over to the other window, checked it and was back in the living room in a half second. He didn't even give himself time to catch his breath, but went into the kitchen to call Casio.

"Where the hell have you been?" his supervisor demanded. "I've been trying to reach you for hours."

Alex ignored his question. "We have a problem," he said quietly. "I had two visitors tonight."

"Damn." The man's anger had vanished. "You okay?"

"Got a lump about the size of Connecticut on the back of my head," he said. "But, otherwise, I'm okay."

"I never expected that strong a reaction," Casio said.

Junior came into the kitchen, causing Alex's stomach to tighten. He'd been trying to talk softly, but obviously not softly enough. He turned toward the outside door, hoping it would muffle his voice.

"I don't think they intended it to happen," he explained. "But that's not the problem. They thought Heather's house was mine. That Heather and I were living together."

"So?"

"Damn it," Alex huffed into the phone. "She's in danger."

"How the hell do you figure she's in danger? You're the one taking out the loans. You're the one gambling."

"What if they come after her to make a point with me?"

"I thought you said there was nothing going on between you two," Casio said.

But Alex barely heard him. Through the window in the door, he could see the street—and the car moving slowly down it, lights off. Was it his imagination or was it slowing down as it passed his house and Heather's?

Heather picked the book up from the living room floor, then reached over to turn the lamp off. The room was filled with the faint early light of dawn, but she could still see Alex asleep on the sofa, Junior resting on the floor next to him and Bonnie tucked in by Alex's arm. It was enough to bring a tear to Heather's eye.

This was an Alex no one ever saw, one that most wouldn't even believe existed. Yet she had been given a peek at this other side of him when she'd seen him with Bonnie, and now she knew for certain that secret, gentler self really did exist.

She'd come out to check on him an hour or so ago, only to get a lecture that he was fine. Typical macho tough-guy attitude. But she wouldn't be fooled by it any longer.

She thought back to the Alex she knew as a young boy. He had loved baseball and climbing trees and doing anything with his dad. She remembered seeing them play catch in the backyard, washing the car together, even shoveling the snow together. He hadn't been looking for adventure then.

It was after his father had died of cancer that Alex'd changed. That he'd become the macho tough guy, accepting every dare, living every moment on the edge. Always needing to be the center of attention, as if he were afraid that no one would like him otherwise. Did he still feel that way, or had he just gotten so used to the excitement that he thought he couldn't live without it?

She thought about that phone call last night—actually she'd been thinking of little else since she'd heard it. All of Alex's wild ways, his flirting with danger was going to come to a head soon. What would he do when she warned him? She frowned, knowing full well what he'd do.

Tough guy Alex would tough it out. He'd pretend it didn't matter, that everything was fine. That he could handle it.

And that gentle side of him would be buried deeper and deeper until it wouldn't even slip through in moments like this. Was there a way to save Alex from himself? Was there a way to free him from his craving for excitement so that the gentler side of him could be given a chance?

She must have sighed or stirred or made some slight sound for little Bonnie lifted her head and yawned. Heather smiled at her in spite of her worries. The tiny kitten had come so far from the frightened little feral cat that she and Alex had rescued two weeks ago. Once Bonnie had dared to trust—

An idea suddenly took hold of Heather's mind. Did she dare? It was truly outrageous, but it also might be the only way to save Alex. And he had agreed with the principle last night. Of course they had been talking about Bonnie, but agreeing was agreeing.

Dorothy put the last clip in her hair and stepped back to look at the effect in the mirror. Yuck. She needed to look sophisticated, yet casually so. Parisian. This was an art gallery that drew in tourists. She couldn't look like one.

That was probably the whole trouble. She still looked like a tourist so the locals were just being touristy friendly to her, not friendly friendly. And there were so many bistros and cafés to visit, she probably just hadn't found the one that was right for her, that had the people in it that would be her new friends. No, she just had to be patient and give herself time. This would start to feel like home soon.

The shrill ringing of the phone split the silence, much to her amazement. Who in the world would be calling her? Brad and Penny had left Paris last week. She stared at the instrument for a long moment as if expecting it to be some sort of prank.

It could be her new boss at the art gallery. Maybe he didn't want her to work there after all. Oh, that would be all she needed. She tossed the hair clips onto the dresser and scrambled over the bed for the phone.

"Dorothy?"

"Heather?" Dorothy sat down on the edge of the bed in disbelief.

"Hey, I promised to stay in touch."

"Yeah, but—" Dorothy looked at her watch, for some unknown reason still set at Chesterton time. "But it's barely five o'clock in the morning there."

"I always get up early. And I thought this would be early for you. Penny said everyone in Paris stays up all night so I thought you wouldn't get up until the afternoon.''

''Well, not quite everyone.'' Dorothy hoped her laugh hid the reality of her life here. ''How are you? How's everyone there?''

Damn. Heather probably thought she was asking about Toto.

''I'm fine. Everybody's fine.''

Everybody? That was all she got, a generic everybody? ''That's good,'' she said brightly in spite of the tightening of her lips. She frowned at a speck of lint on her skirt and scraped at it. ''I'm really glad to hear it. Brad and Penny get home all right?''

''Oh, yeah. Lots of great stories. It made us all wish we could go to Paris.''

She left the lint alone. ''Us all?''

''You know, Aunty Em and me. Mrs. Fogarty. Nancy Abbott.''

But not Toto. Not that she was surprised or disappointed. She didn't care a bit what he didn't do or where he didn't go.

''How's Junior?'' Dorothy asked, then fell back on the bed in annoyance with herself. Of all the dumb, revealing questions.

''Junior?'' Heather laughed. ''Actually, he's staying with us for a few days.''

There was something in Heather's voice. ''Us?'' Dorothy repeated.

Heather laughed, an off sound that just didn't ring quite true. ''Me and Victoria and Henry and the new kitty, Bonnie.''

''Oh. That must be fun for you all.''

''I guess.'' She paused and Dorothy could feel her

hesitation. "Actually I was calling for a reason. I was wondering if you could help me."

"I'll be glad to try." It must be something awfully important to warrant a transatlantic phone call.

"I was wondering about that cabin you used earlier this summer. You know, the one owned by that couple you met in Florida. I thought you said it was going to be empty all summer and that you could use it whenever you wanted."

"Yes," Dorothy said slowly. "It's in the upper peninsula a bit northwest of a little town called Watton. Why?"

Heather cleared her throat, a sure sign she was embarrassed. "Well, I was wondering if I could use it this weekend."

"You want to rough it in the wilds of northern Michigan?" Timid, mousy Heather wanted to spend a week isolated in the middle of nowhere with erratic electricity and a forest full of things that growled, howled and prowled all night? "Is this really Heather Mahoney or some imposter?"

Heather laughed, a real laugh this time, but then her voice turned serious. "I wasn't actually going by myself," she said carefully. "A friend was going to come with. We just wanted a little time alone and thought a long weekend away would be great."

"I see." And she did. She was surprised, she had to admit. She hadn't thought Heather had anyone special. But she had been gone for several weeks. Things were bound to have changed in that time.

"Not that we'll really be alone," Heather said with a laugh. "Junior's coming along to keep the wildlife away from me, and I've got to take the kitten I'm socializing or I'll be back at square one when I return."

"Of course, you can use the cabin," Dorothy assured her. "Use it for as long as you want. You going up soon?"

"This morning," Heather said. Her voice reflected relief and excitement. "I'm going to skip the teachers' workshops. Well, once I make a quick call to Aunty Em and see if she or Penny can keep an eye on the cats for me."

"I sure hope you have fun."

"Oh, I expect we will."

Dorothy found her heart getting heavier and heavier as she recited the directions, and was downright morose by the time she got off the phone. Her friends were moving on with life without her. It was normal and what she wanted, but sad, too.

Chapter Nine

Alex woke up to the smell of coffee and warm bread. No, those things would make it a dream, so he couldn't be waking up. There was no coffee until he made some and—

He felt faint warm breath in his face and his eyes flew open. He was lying on a sofa with a cat sitting on his chest, staring at him. Last night came rushing back. The confrontation with the thugs. The bump on his head. Heather's stubbornness in bringing him into her house. His driving need for her touch.

The cat fled as Alex started to sit up, which was just as well. Every muscle in his body ached and his head felt ready to explode. But there was a deeper hurt that he couldn't quite locate, a stronger one than the others combined. Just went to show what a bad idea it was to let anyone into his life, even marginally.

"Oh, you're up."

Heather was way across the room standing in the doorway to the kitchen, but her soft voice easily wrapped itself around his aching heart. He looked over at her—his heart as fearful as it was eager—and his eyes drank in her gentleness, the beauty of her smile and the warmth in her eyes. Just looking at her made him feel better. Stronger. More alive.

She was so beautiful, even in simple shorts and a T-shirt. Like a fragile flower. And her delicate innocence made his world seem all the more sordid. All the more dirty. All the more necessary that he protect her and keep her safe.

"How are you feeling?" she asked.

"Fine. Great."

He got to his feet with gusto, ignoring the screaming protests of his stiff muscles. He'd made a decision during the long hours of last night, and seeing her this morning only brought back the urgency of it all. He had to get her away from here. A few months out of town would be perfect. A few weeks, pretty good. But for now he'd settle for a long weekend. It would be time enough to convince Casio that she needed protection.

She turned from the doorway, disappearing into the kitchen. "I hope I didn't wake you up," she called back to him. "I tried to be quiet."

"I didn't hear you at all," he said, watching the doorway for her return. "I'm just not a late sleeper."

He told himself that he didn't miss her, that that ache in the region of his heart was the result of sleeping on this short sofa. He just needed to stretch the kinks out. Good idea. Bending down, he put his hands on the floor and stretched his leg muscles.

It probably would have been better if he'd stayed

awake as he had intended to. Stayed up and kept watch. He knew that was unrealistic—he had needed sleep—but he didn't like the vulnerability that sleep brought. And it wasn't just the fact the thugs had been by last night. He had never liked sleeping when someone else was moving around.

"How's your head?" Heather was back with a cup of coffee. "Do you want cream or sugar? I just brought it black."

"The head's fine." He straightened up. "And black is great. Just how I like it." How had she known? Not that it mattered. He took the cup gratefully and sipped at the steaming liquid. "This is a luxury."

She'd been starting back toward the kitchen, but frowned at him over her shoulder. "How so?"

"I don't get coffee served to me at home." He followed her into the other room.

"Want some breakfast or do you want to shower first?"

"I'll shower when I get back home," he said. "I'll just clean up a little here, if you don't mind." There were some things they had to discuss.

"Of course, I don't mind," she said with a snap to her voice. "And I'm not sure you ought to be going home. Unless it's just to get clean clothes."

She took his breath away. A small, fragile-looking woman with red cheeks and fiery eyes. Ready to go to war over his well-being. He didn't know what it was— her passion or her beauty—but it bowled him over. He wanted nothing more than to take her in his arms and hold her.

No, he wanted more than that. Much more. He wanted to make love to her, over and over again. He wanted to feel her warmth surround him and be lost in her womanliness. But surprisingly, he wanted even more. He had such a craving for her tenderness that it almost scared him.

It had to be the knock he'd taken to his head. That and the few hours of sleep he got. He helped himself to another cup of coffee, then turned toward her. "Want a refill?"

"Sure."

He filled her cup, noticing the faint floral scent about her, but not letting it trouble him. Just as the soft moistness of her lips did not draw him. He put the coffeepot back on the coffeemaker and sat down at the table.

"I can't believe it's almost Labor Day," he said. "I'm really looking forward to the long weekend."

"Me, too," she said and then got to her feet. "What would you like for breakfast? Toast? Cereal? Bacon and eggs?"

"Toast would be great," he said. "So have you got any plans for the weekend? Hey, I bet it would be a good time to go visit your folks in Arizona," he added as if the idea had just occurred to him.

"Actually," she started, her voice slow, uncertain. "Actually, I was supposed to go up to the upper peninsula to help Ida Crawford close her cabin up for the season and then drive her back home like I always do."

"And why aren't you?"

"Toto was going to drive me up there and then Ida and I would come back in her car on Monday, but it turns out Toto's pulled an extra shift and can't do it."

"Is that all?" Alex practically laughed aloud. "Heck, I can fix that. I can drive you up there."

"I thought I was going to drive," Alex said, trying again to find a comfortable position in the passenger seat. There wasn't one. Every position he tried in the past three hours had put him too close to Heather to think clearly. Maybe he should have had Junior sit in the front and he take the back with Bonnie and her carrier.

"If I remember correctly," Heather told him, "you got a severe bump to your head last night. And a concussion is nothing to joke about."

"The concussion is your diagnosis, not mine."

None of this was turning out the way he had envisioned. They should have taken his car which was built for speed, not Heather's standard-model sedan. Except that his had somehow acquired a flat tire overnight. And he would have left Junior and Bonnie at home, in spite of Heather's insistence that she had promised to dog-sit Junior and Bonnie's socialization couldn't be interrupted. The animals would slow them down if trouble found them.

And he definitely should be driving. He was the one trained in evasive maneuvers. He was the one who could push a car to its maximum. He was the one who could spot danger before it spotted them. All reasons why he should be at the wheel. But Heather wouldn't hear of it.

"It would have been the doctor's diagnosis too, if you'd've let me take you to the emergency room." Heather carefully passed a slow-moving semitrailer truck, then got back into the right-hand lane. "Besides, I'm a good driver. I've never been in an accident and never even got a ticket."

She reached over to adjust the air-conditioning, her hand coming all too close to his knee. Just a little farther and she would—

He moved his leg and forced his thoughts back to this whole issue of protection. "So, tell me about this cabin. Where's it at exactly?"

"Exactly?" She glanced at him, her blue eyes dark with confusion. "You mean, like latitude and longitude?"

His thoughts tried to stray back to those eyes of hers, and other things that might make them darken. Fear. Wonder. Passion. But he pulled his attention back to business. There had been a note in her voice that tightened his nerves a notch. Could she be hiding something or was he getting paranoid?

"Is the cabin in Watton or out in the country?" he asked.

"It's in the country," she said. "But then, Watton is pretty much country itself."

And what did that mean? He let his glance linger over her for a moment—but in a professional way. Heather was soft and gentle and trusting. A teddy bear pajama person. To her, country would be baby raccoons and fireflies at dusk. Finding wildflowers blooming among the stones of a shallow creek and nights so dark you could wish on even the dimmest stars.

Country was a whole different matter to him. Space. Lots and lots of space with lots and lots of places to hide. Sparsely populated. A few overworked police officers covering vast square miles of space. "County police protection," he muttered. Response time measured in hours instead of minutes.

"County police?" She sounded confused, then laughed. "I guess so. But that doesn't mean they're any less trained than a city policeman."

She just didn't understand. The bad feeling in his stomach grew. Damn. He didn't like any of this. He definitely should have asked more questions before he'd agreed to take her up there. He just wasn't thinking clearly around her and that had to change. As of right now.

"There are neighbors close by, aren't there?" he asked.

She flashed him a smile—whose potent rays he deflected—then went back to her driving. "Boy, you sure are full of questions. You'd think you had something dastardly planned and wanted to make sure there were no witnesses."

"Hardly." Her nonanswer meant no neighbors. If there were any, she would have said so.

He turned to glare out the side window, fighting back his anger at himself. He couldn't believe how stupid he had been, jumping at this plan without thinking it through. He'd wanted to see Heather away from Chesterton so when this chance presented itself, he'd grabbed it, no questions asked. It had seemed perfect, ready-made. Harmless. He bit back a silent curse. He'd made it sound exactly that when he'd called Casio on his cell phone this morning from the bathroom while he was supposedly showering.

"I'm taking her up to a friend's cabin someplace near Watton in the upper peninsula," he'd told his supervisor. "She'll be safe up there and I'll be back in action tomorrow evening."

"This really necessary?" Casio'd asked.

"Yes. For her and for my peace of mind."

But just where had that mind of his been? He glanced once more at the cars behind them, but everything was as before. Ordinary folks going about their business. No one speeding up, no one dropping back. It could mean something or nothing.

"I don't like the feel of this at all," he told Heather. "This cabin is too isolated to be safe."

"You really know how to set a person's mind at ease." Her laugh was nervous. "Maybe you should just stay up there, too."

A little part of him found the idea appealing, but he broke it off quickly. He was the reason for Heather's problems. He was the honey that was drawing the scum.

"Maybe we should just collect Ida and come right back down." No, then Heather'd be back in harm's way. "Or better yet, you and Ida can find a nice hotel in Mackinaw and spend the weekend there."

"Why, when we've got a cabin all paid for?"

She just wasn't understanding. How much was he going to have to spell out for her? He was trying to warn her, not terrify her. "Because it's safer, that's why," he snapped. "You never know—"

There was movement and then a low growl from the back seat. Great. Junior was getting ticked at him. They'd never been the best of friends and things weren't getting any better.

"It's okay, Junior," Heather said soothingly over her shoulder. Then she turned back to Alex. "Look, I know what I'm doing and it's for the best. It's what has to be done. But what do you say we save our arguments until we get up there?"

Alex bit back his argument. She was right; it would be better to wait. If the cabin was as isolated as he expected, he'd be able to show her the dangers more easily than he could describe them now.

The problem was he had lost control somewhere along the way. He'd had a plan to protect her and it got too mixed up with her plan to go help Ida Crawford. He had to bring them back to his plan, then everything would be fine.

"Do you wonder where all these cars are going?" she asked glancing out the car window.

He turned to stare at her, then back out at the cars. "I guess. In a way." Though maybe not with the same innocent wonder that she had.

He turned back to her. Alex felt a need to know what went on behind Heather's sky-blue eyes. What did she want from life?

"Are you jealous of those hurrying off to exciting places?" he asked her.

"Not at all," she said. "I like my life. I love teaching the little kids and making costumes in my free time. I love coming home to my cats and finding good homes for my strays. I wouldn't trade my life for another."

She spoke with such passion, such surety. As if she knew what mattered and had it in her hands. Her fervor left a longing in its wake. He let his gaze go back to the traffic, but he couldn't release the uncertainty that was suddenly nagging at him.

"You're lucky," he told her.

"Why? Don't you like your life?"

What a question! He loved his life. He loved the adventure, the danger, the need to belong everywhere and nowhere. Yet strange and unbidden memories were coming forward, like a book falling open at an unexpected spot.

"I think my father hated his life," he said slowly. "He never exactly said so, but I could tell."

"What makes you think that?"

Alex shrugged. How could you explain something

that was always felt but never expressed? "He had such dreams."

"Having dreams doesn't mean you hate the present," Heather pointed out. "It just means you have something you want to do in the future."

Once he started telling her, the words just seemed unable to stop. "Everything he wanted to do, he put off. He wanted to learn to fly. To race motorcycles. To do deep-sea diving. And he died before he had a chance to do any of it. He kept saying he could do them all tomorrow, but then he never had a tomorrow."

"And you're trying to give him one," Heather said.

He frowned at her, looking for something deep in her eyes and only half hearing her words. "What's that supposed to mean?"

"Nothing," she said. "Just that he made his own choices. Maybe he liked the quieter life more than you think."

She'd wanted him to take a peek at his life, but it wasn't his life she'd shown him. It was somebody else's. His was good, satisfying, what he wanted. And if he'd gotten off track lately, it was only a temporary thing.

"What are you saying?" he asked. "That I'm just using my father as an excuse to lead a wild life? Is that why you won't let me drive, because you think I'm reckless?"

"I won't let you drive because you had a concussion and your reflexes are liable to be off."

Alex just watched her for a long moment, caught in an emotional landslide. Longing. Indecision. Regret. Determination. Why had he opened himself up to her like that? It left him feeling weak and vulnerable, even if her conclusions were all nonsense.

He needed to get back to being himself. He needed to be in control again.

It was early evening by the time Heather pulled the car into the parking spot in front of the Watton grocery store and turned off the motor. Rain was spattering against the windshield, making the outside world as blurry as her inside one. She was tired, achy from sitting, and thoroughly tensed up from thinking about what she'd tell Alex when they got to the cabin.

Her nerves had tightened with every mile she'd driven and she hadn't been able to hide the fact. Luckily, Alex had thought she was just nervous about driving over the Mackinaw Bridge and still nervous about it when they stopped for dinner in Saint Ignace.

Little did he know. The bridge was no big deal. She wasn't a bridge-a-phobic or whatever they were called. No, she was an anger-a-phobic. She didn't like having other people angry with her. In less than an hour Alex would find out what this was all about. And Heather knew he was going to be really mad.

She looked up at the small Watton grocery store and unbuckled her seat belt. "I need to pick up a few things. You want to come in?"

"Of course," he said, as if he couldn't even understand her asking.

Rats. It's not that she didn't want him there, but it would have been all right if he had declined the invitation. A little time to herself—to catch her breath and work up her courage—would be awfully nice.

"Okay." She checked on Junior and Bonnie and

both seemed fine. ''It's just a few more miles, babies. Then you'll have room to move around.''

After taking a deep enough breath to fill a hot air balloon, she stepped out of the car and into the drizzling rain. It wasn't enough to cool her off, though. Alex was waiting at the door of the grocery, sending her heart into a definite stutter. There ought to be a law against men being so tall and handsome. And certainly against them being so unaffected by her touch.

He held open the screen door for her. ''So, what are we getting?''

''Oh, odds and ends for the weekend.'' She stopped inside the door and looked around, hoping she could find seclusion down its aisles by sending Alex over to get the peanut butter while she got the jelly.

No such luck. It was a typical little country general store, tiny in size but carrying everything—Elvis Presley videos to garden hoses to mustard. There was no room left for her to hide even for a moment.

''Howdy, folks,'' the old man from behind the counter said.

Heather hurried over. If she couldn't literally hide from Alex, maybe she could mentally hide from him.

''We need some food for the weekend,'' she told the proprietor and pulled out her list. ''Where are the canned soups?''

''Last aisle at the far end,'' he said.

Heather nodded, then she and her list scooted to the last aisle.

''So you folks come up for the holiday?'' the old man asked. ''Too bad the rains had to come on your long weekend.''

Heather's step grew a little lighter as she realized he was talking to Alex. She would have the aisle to herself! She could crouch down behind the lima beans and give herself a pep talk.

"Yeah," she heard Alex say. "But we're just up here to help Ida Crawford close up her cabin. Not really for a vacation."

Good. Have a nice long conversation about the weather, Heather told them silently. The rain didn't bother her at all. It was actually rather prophetic, she thought. Sometimes what you needed wasn't what you wanted, be it rain instead of sunshine or—

"Ida Crawford?" the old man was saying. "She new around here?"

The words interrupted Heather's meditation with a solid jolt. She grabbed a couple of cans of soup and hurried back up to the front of the store, hauling in a couple of cans of tuna and a bottle of salad dressing along the way.

"I don't think so," Alex said. "She comes up here every year."

"Huh." The old man picked at his teeth with a toothpick. "We got a Isa Davenport over in Baraga County, but I sure don't know of any Ida Crawford."

Heather dumped her items on the counter. "Actually, her cabin's not very close," she said quickly. She glanced Alex's way but he didn't look overly suspicious. "She's north of Route 28."

"Oh, yeah?" He rubbed his chin. "Don't recall much up north but that Florida rich folks' cabin, and ain't nobody been there this year 'cepting mice and raccoons."

Mice and raccoons? Heather gulped back an onrush of fear. Nothing that Junior and Bonnie couldn't handle, right? "Well, actually it's way north. Way way north. And I probably have the road wrong."

Heather knew Alex was looking at her strangely by this time. He had to be. She must sound like a demented homing pigeon. But she was going through with this, come hell or high water. Or Alex's suspicions.

"Want to grab a quart of orange juice?" she asked him, then went over to pick out a couple of small baskets of fresh fruit and salad fixings. She put them on the counter. "I think that's everything."

The old man started to ring up the items on his old brass cash register, bagging them far too slowly for Heather's liking. She didn't want Alex to start questioning the route or her plans or anything. He came over to her side, a frown that almost reached to the South Pole on his face.

"Are you sure—"

"That I've got everything?" she finished for him. "I didn't need much. I've got some stuff in a cooler in the car."

Heather counted out the money and shoved the bags into Alex's arms in record time. Too bad exiting grocery stores wasn't an Olympic event. "Thanks for everything."

With a bright smile, she tugged on Alex's arm, practically pulling him toward the door.

"Hope you two find the right cabin," the man called after them.

"We will," Heather called back.

Once she and Alex were outside and back in the rain, she let go of his arm and fought to hide her sigh of relief. One hurdle down.

"Are you sure of the way?" Alex asked.

Heather just marched ahead of him, going over to unlock the trunk. "You mean because of that sweet old man?'' She forced a loud laugh. "Would you believe I stop here every year and he always says the same thing? He always forgets about Ida because she's just a summer resident. He only remembers the year-round folks.''

Alex put the bags into the trunk, then Heather closed it with a solid thunk. "Well, let's get going. We want to get there by dark.''

Alex got back in the car and Heather took advantage of the moment's separation to wipe her sweaty hands on her rain-dampened shorts. How was she getting to be such a good liar? Now, if only she was as good at disabling cars, though Aunty Em's suggestion for letting the air out of Alex's tire worked. Heather had to trust that her other suggestion would, too. And trust that her nervous stomach wouldn't get any nervouser.

"Heather?'' Alex called. "Is something wrong?''

She started, then hurried into the car. "Just breathing in the fresh country air.''

She didn't check to see if he was giving her any kind of look at all, but pulled back onto the road. This was it. She was really doing it. After resetting the trip odometer, she clutched the steering wheel tightly and kept an eye out for the stone bridge Dorothy had told her about, then she turned onto the dirt road that appeared amid the dense pines. Dorothy had called the road a seasonal two track, and now Heather knew just what that meant—two tracks through the weeds and only passable in the good seasons. Luckily the rains hadn't been that heavy.

"Damn. I hope we don't meet any other traffic,'' Alex said as branches brushed the windows. "There's barely room for one vehicle here.''

"I don't think many people come this way." She hoped not anyway.

"I can't believe Ida comes up here," he added. "You really need a Jeep or four-wheel-drive truck for this road."

"Oh, it's not so bad."

She was trembling, and her reactions were so far off, that she was sure she was making the road seem much worse than it was. It's true that the lane was dotted with puddles and overgrown with bushes and weeds hanging in the way. But it was her alternating between hitting a puddle-filled pothole too fast and slamming on the brakes too fast that was giving them whiplash. And it didn't help that she jumped every time a branch snapped back at the windows as if it were alive.

"Just how far is this cabin?" Alex asked.

"Another few miles." Okay, another eight miles. But he didn't want the real truth. And besides, it wasn't like there was a place to turn around and go back, even if she wanted to.

Another mile, maybe two and they drove through a partial clearing. The trees were thin enough that the sky was visible above them. Unfortunately, it meant the rain had come through at full strength earlier. A huge puddle covered the track.

Heather held her breath as she hit it, feeling the wheels pull slightly at the mud, but after a long scary moment they kept on going. Maybe that was too bad. If they got stuck in the mud, that would be the reason they had to stay here and she wouldn't have to confess her plan to Alex. Of course, they would have to walk another few miles to the cabin and that wouldn't be fun.

"I don't like this at all," he snapped as they went

under the cover of the trees again. "We're collecting Ida and then we're leaving. This is beyond remote. The county police would be no protection at all. They'd never get here in time in an emergency."

She just kept on driving. What was the matter with him? He had turned into a prophet of gloom and doom. "Why are you always worrying something's going to happen?" she asked. "This is the country. It's safe out here."

"You can't really believe that. This would be a perfect place to hide out. Or to ambush somebody."

Heather felt a sudden stab of understanding. That call she'd overheard last night, that man had threatened Alex. He hadn't heard the message since she'd erased his answering machine tape when they'd gone to his house this morning for him to shower and collect clean clothes, but he knew they would be after him. And was worrying now about where they would catch up with him.

"They'd have to know where someone was in order to ambush them," she pointed out. And no one in Chesterton knew where they were going. Only Dorothy did and she certainly wasn't going to tell.

"Or they'd have to catch him unawares," Alex added, sounding as if he were talking more to himself than her.

"Right." She had no idea what he was talking about, but since it seemed to satisfy something in him, she wasn't going to question.

She had other things to think about anyway, like whether they would get there before dark. The shadows were deepening yet the track seemed to go on endlessly. She glanced at the trip odometer. They were almost there, thank goodness.

A low-hanging tree branch swiped at the windshield, then suddenly the cabin appeared ahead of them. It was a small boxlike building huddled under the pines, rough-hewn siding with a wide, welcoming front porch that did nothing to hide its empty look. Heather drove the car across the pine needles up close to the house, her stomach a tight ball of nerves. This was it. Time to face the firing squad.

"Are you sure there's somebody here?" Alex said. His voice sounded suspicious and more than a touch angry.

"There's got to be." Her nervous laugh came real easy. "Maybe you need to look around."

He gave her a look, his eyes dark and dangerous. She'd never seen him that way before and her stomach tensed up even further. He looked about as far from a literature professor as possible right now, and soon that angry look would be directed at her.

"You just stay here," he ordered and got out of the car, watching all around him as he did so.

Heather's heart crept up into her throat so breathing was almost impossible. She watched as he walked carefully over to the house. It wasn't too late. She could just tell him it was a mistake and they could go. He'd be annoyed, but that would be all.

He disappeared around the corner of the house and Junior whined softly, nudging her shoulder with his nose. She thought of Alex in that awful neighborhood in Chicago where he'd gotten mugged. And last night when someone had been after him. No, she was not going to chicken out. Alex was in trouble and this was going to give him a chance.

Taking a deep breath, she bent down and pulled the cover off the car's fuse box. Holy cow, there was a dozen of them here! Aunty Em said to take the ignition fuse, but which one was that? Heather popped her head up and glanced around the car. Alex was still out of sight. She dove down again and just pulled all the fuses out. Better safe than sorry.

Then she sat up, keeping one eye out for Alex as she dumped all the fuses into a little plastic bag and sealed it up.

"You have to help me out here," she told Junior and reached around the seat to get at his collar. "Under no circumstances are you to let him have these."

Junior just sat still as she unbuckled his heavy leather collar, duct-taped the fuses to it, and put it back on. It was done. She breathed a heavy sigh, then climbed out of the car. The rain had stopped and the air smelled of wet earth and pine. It really was very pretty here, a secluded little paradise. The rest of the world might not exist, for all she could tell. It was a wonderful spot to spend the weekend. Hopefully Alex would agree— sooner or later.

She let Junior out of the car and went around to get Bonnie's carrier. "Come on, sweetie. I bet you're tired of being cooped up in here. Let's get you into the house."

Carrying the cat carrier and a box of supplies, she climbed the steps and opened the door. It was open, just as Dorothy had said it would be. Junior raced up to join her and she let him go in first. A musty, dusty closed-up smell rushed out to greet her.

The cabin looked no larger inside than it had from the outside. A small living room was furnished with rough wooden furniture and a stone fireplace graced the far wall. Beyond that was a kitchen. To her right— she peeked in—was the bedroom. The only bedroom.

Her face flushed as she turned back to the sofa. It was short, and very hard-looking. Now what? She hadn't even thought about sleeping arrangements. What a dummy she was! Did she offer to sleep in the car?

Bonnie protested her confinement and Heather shook off her dilemma. Other things to worry about first.

She opened the carrier so Bonnie could come out when she dared and fixed her litter box, then poured some water she'd brought from home into a big dish for both Bonnie and Junior. While the animals were investigating their supplies, Heather went over to the west end of the living room. As she was pulling aside the curtains to let in the last rays of the sun, she heard Alex's steps on the porch. She turned toward the door, her heart all but stopping.

"Heather?" He pushed open the door, his face looking like thunder about to crash. "I thought I said to stay in the car."

She shrugged and wiped her hands nervously on her shorts. "They needed to get out," she said, waving at the animals. "It was a long drive."

His frown didn't lessen as he looked around. "This place is deserted," he pointed out sharply. "There's no sign of Ida or any other human being."

"No?" Heather shrugged. "I guess she didn't come up after all."

"She didn't come?" Even though his voice was quiet, it seemed close to a bellow.

Junior looked up, a soft growl in his throat. Alex just glared at the dog, then back at Heather. "I think we'd better get out of here while there's still some light left,'' he said. ''If we go now, we should get almost to the road before it's really dark.''

She clenched her hands behind her back, steeling her whole self as if preparing to take a blow. ''No,'' she said.

He'd bent down to pick up the water dish, and stopped. The look of thunder in his face deepened. It set Heather's knees trembling and stole every drop of moisture in her mouth.

''No?'' he repeated.

She shook her head, trying to find a way to speak. ''No.'' It came out hoarse and gravelly, but audible. ''We're staying the weekend here. It's for your own good.''

Chapter Ten

"What the hell are you talking about?" Alex snapped. Something was going on here, something that felt like a stupid game. And he had never liked games.

Heather was standing in the middle of this dusty, dirty, deserted cabin, trying to look brave and failing. Her blue eyes were wide with worry and she kept biting at her bottom lip. His anger faltered a bit under her nervous regard.

"We're staying here," she said with enough bravado to look him right in the eye. Her voice was strained, but clear enough. "You and I. Away from all temptations and evil influences."

"Evil influences?" He felt as if he had stumbled into someone else's dream and it irritated the hell out of him. He didn't have time for this. "What are you talking about?"

"You have a serious gambling habit, Alex. Don't bother to deny it. I know you do."

"No, I—" He stopped. Damn. He couldn't defend himself without breaking his cover and he couldn't do that. "So what if I do? What does that have to do—" He paused, understanding coming slowly. "Ida Crawford never was up here, was she? You made it all up."

Heather nodded. "You needed a place to stay where there would be no temptations. And this seemed perfect."

The pieces were falling in place, though he could hardly believe what picture they were forming. "You brought me up here so I wouldn't gamble?"

"Not just gambling," she told him. "So you could see that you don't need constant excitement to be happy."

This was unbelievable. He was in the middle of a huge undercover investigation and innocent Heather was giving him more trouble than all the crooks put together.

"I'm not staying," he pointed out.

"You have to. I'm not letting you leave."

The idea that she could stop him was laughable, but he was polite enough not to. "Heather, keeping me up here isn't going to stop me from gambling. I can gamble any place I am. All I have to do is pick up the phone and call a bookie."

"If you had a phone," she said amiably. Too amiably.

Double damn. The hell with being polite. "What did you do with my cell phone?" he snapped.

"Nothing," she said. "It's perfectly fine. Just sitting on your dresser back home. I took it out of your bag while you were getting your razor from the bathroom."

"You what?"

Junior growled, and Alex took a step back. Not that he needed the warning, but he sure needed the space to get himself under control. He could not believe she had done that.

"You mean we're up here in this godforsaken place without a phone? What if something happens and we need help?"

"I have my cell phone," she told him. "But it needs a security code to be used."

Thank goodness. At least they weren't without some basic protection. He took a deep breath and tried to think rationally. It was time to regroup.

"Heather, I appreciate your concern," he said carefully. "But I really don't need your help."

"Denial will do you no good," she replied. "You can't get better until you admit you have a problem."

He just stared at her, then sank onto the sofa. If he spoke, he would shout and Junior would growl and Heather would get even more stubborn. There had to be a way to convince her. Maybe he should—

"You're overdue on a loan," she said. "You were lucky last night, but that doesn't mean you will be next time."

"How—" He swallowed all his arguments hard. She must have heard them talking in front of her house. Damn. She knew there was violence involved and still let herself get caught up in this. Why? The Heather he knew should be at home hiding. Why was she trying to rescue him?

Oh, no. This time it really became clear. "Heather, I am not some cat needing rescue."

"You need help."

This was unbelievable. They were getting out of here even if he had to drag her.

"Come on," he said. "We're going back home."

"I don't think so."

"I'm going out to start the car," he said. "Give me the keys, please."

She just kept looking at him, those wide eyes still trying to save him. Except, hell, he didn't need saving. Then she held out the keys.

He took them, feeling almost bad about all this. She meant well, he knew. It wasn't her fault that she was judging things on appearances and didn't know the reality. But still, he had a job to do and he needed to be back in Indiana to get it done. And she needed to be in a safe location, not a deserted cabin in the middle of nowhere. He turned and walked toward the door. No one else moved.

"Are you coming with me?" he asked.

"No."

"Heather, I don't have time to play games."

"I'm not playing."

"I'm going to start the car and if you're not out in thirty seconds, I'm coming back."

"I expect you will."

She didn't look any less nervous, but there was something too calm and assured about her. He eyed her suspiciously, then looked down at the car keys. Had she given him the wrong ones? No, they were the same set she'd driven up here with.

"Want me to take Bonnie's stuff out?" he asked.

"No, thank you," she said. "She's fine where she is."

"I'm not leaving you up here."

"I never thought you would."

This was getting them nowhere. He pulled open the door and stomped across the dirt yard to the car. He'd get it started and show her he meant business. Then she'd let him help her pack up the animals and start back.

He climbed into the car and pushed the horn, just to make a point. It didn't make a point because it didn't make a sound. Not even a squeak.

Damn. He jammed the key into the ignition and turned it. The silence was deafening.

Double damn. He tried again.

Nothing. Not a squeak or a flicker or a flutter. Nothing.

Alex flung the car door open and strode over to the front of the car. After popping the hood, he stared at the motor. In the rapidly fading light, nothing looked unplugged or missing. He jiggled some wires, just to do something, and tried the motor again. Still nothing. The horn still wouldn't make a sound and the lights didn't work. She did something with the electrical system. Rats.

He looked under the hood again. The battery was there so it had to be the fuses.

He went back into the car and looked under the dashboard for the fuse box. He didn't like what he didn't see. It was almost dark in the car, but he didn't need light to see there was no fuses there.

Hell. He slammed the car door and stomped back into the house. Heather was putting some dry food out for the two animals, but stood back up when he came in.

"You took the fuses out of the car. Give them to me, please."

"I don't have them."

He really didn't need this. It was bad enough that they'd be driving all night, but he at least wanted to get out of this rugged area while it was still light.

"Just give me the fuses or tell me where you put them."

"Junior has them."

Alex looked at the dog who was sitting on his haunches, grinning at him. It was still light enough in the room for him to see something was taped to the beast's collar. But Alex took only a half step toward the dog before he started his low growl again. Alex stopped.

Heather came over to put her hand on his arm, her eyes pools of caring and concern. "I know that we're not going to totally cure you of your gambling addiction, but we need to stay here long enough to make a good start on it. We're not leaving until I'm satisfied you're on the road to recovery."

A tiny meow caused Alex to turn. Apparently Bonnie wanted to warn him how stubborn Heather could be.

Alex sighed. Well, Heather wasn't the only stubborn one here. Yeah, she had him boxed in right now. But that was only because he hadn't realized what kind of game she was playing. Now that he knew the rules, nothing was going to hold him back. He was going to get her out of here and somewhere safe.

"How are we going to know when I'm ready to leave?" he asked.

"I'll know and, in the meantime, Junior's going to hold the fuses."

"What if I try to take them?" Alex said.

Heather smiled sweetly. "I imagine he'll just rip you to shreds."

The dog was grinning at them both, but he only gave Heather his adoring look. Since Junior was a trained police dog Alex doubted the beast could be persuaded to transfer his allegiance. Although, it might be worth a try. And Alex did know Junior's weak spot—beer. He'd roll over and play dead for a can of suds. Lately Toto had him on near beer.

"Man, am I thirsty." Alex stretched his arms high over his head. "We got any beer in the place?"

Heather didn't even bother to grin. She just laughed out loud. "Not a drop."

Damn. That store in Watton was ten miles back. On this terrain that was a three-hour walk. He might get it closer to two if he ran, but if Heather told Junior to, he would run Alex down and drag him back before he even reached the property line.

"I'll be glad to make some lemonade," Heather said.

His first inclination was to tell her to forget it, but getting into a spitting match wouldn't solve the problem and neither would telling her this was for her own good. He was going to have to play it by ear and see what developed. Something would present itself. Some weakness, some preference that he could exploit. For her sake, he couldn't give up, no matter what he had to pretend.

"Maybe later," he said tightly. "I'd better unload the car while we still have a little bit of light."

"This is going to be great," Heather told him, giving his arm a squeeze. "You'll see."

He just nodded and turned to the door, stopping at a small sound near his foot. Bonnie was there, chattering quietly. He had the feeling she was giving him advice on how to survive Heather's forced-socialization.

"Hey, kid," he said to her. "How are you and Junior getting along? Think you could get something off his collar for me?"

Heather took the lemonade mix and a pitcher from the box she had brought in from the car. She wasn't at all discouraged by Alex's reaction; it was what she had expected. This really was no different than socializing the cats. They didn't like being caught and fought against it, just as he had. But little by little, the cats stopped fighting and learned to like being touched and held and loved. Then it didn't take long to win them over.

"Of course, that's not what I'm trying to do with Alex," she pointed out to Junior. The very thought of touching and holding him made her whole body blush. "I just want him to see that there are other ways to be happy. He doesn't need to risk his safety and livelihood."

Other ways...like loving and being loved? The blush turned to fire and she hurried toward the kitchen. Now that Alex had been "caught," the next thing was to give him a reward. Something to show him how good this risk-free life could be.

"No, it's not going to have anything to do with touching," she told Junior, just in case the dog was getting ideas. "I was thinking of lemonade and brownies right out of the microwave."

She stopped in the kitchen doorway, feeling around the doorway for the light switch. She couldn't feel one.

She turned, and looked all around the doorway and

beyond. Sometimes the wiring in old houses was really creative and the switches could be in odd places.

But there wasn't one near the door, or next to the pantry. Not even by the table. She frowned, clutching the lemonade mix and pitcher to her chest as she looked all over. Not only could she not find the light switches, she couldn't see any lights! Could someone have broken in and stolen them?

Suddenly she was seeing light-fixture-bearing hoodlums huddled in the shadows. Brigands with lamp fetishes lurking beyond the stove, ready to skewer her with a fluorescent bulb. Her mouth went dry as she took a step back. Behind her, Alex came in with another load from the car.

"Alex?" she called out.

There was a loud thump of a box being dropped heavily, then he was in the doorway. The anger and annoyance that had been there earlier was replaced by concern. "What's the matter?"

She felt silly then, faced with his strength and ferocity. "Uh, I wondered if you could turn on the lights for me," she said. "My hands are full."

"Turn the lights on?" He looked around. "That'll be a trick. It doesn't look like the place has electricity."

"No electricity?"

Oh, no. That meant no microwave and so no microwave brownies. What was she going to do for his reward? She had to reward him, it was absolutely necessary in the socialization process. Bonnie would never have come around if Heather hadn't given her a treat right after she'd been caught.

"A bummer, right?" Alex said, his voice a little too casual. "I can't imagine not having any electricity. No coffeemaker making coffee before we get up. No radio to listen to." He paused, then went on. "Can't even have a night-light."

Part of her was disappointed, and another part was worried, but still another part was so relieved at his words she could have hugged him. He was following the predictable pattern. The feral cat kept fighting even after it was caught and so was Alex. But his combative attitude would lessen after his reward. And she could still give him one. She'd bought some cookies in Watton. They would have cookies and lemonade.

"Who needs a night-light?" she asked with a laugh. After putting down the lemonade mix and pitcher on the kitchen table, she went over and opened the pantry. Dishes. Linens. Boxes of supplies.

"There must be some form of light here," she said. "A lantern. Candles. I have a little flashlight in my purse but I doubt the batteries will last all weekend."

"Even if there's something there, it might not work. And we can't stay here in the dark," he said. "We'll use your flashlight to put the fuses back in—"

"Aha! Candles," Heather cried and pulled a box out of a kitchen cabinet.

"Yeah, but—"

"And matches!" She held a little box in the air triumphantly. Ha. Had he really thought she would give in so quickly? She had tamed wilder beasts than he.

She fit a candle in a holder on the shelf, then lit it. A soft warm glow washed over them, a faint flickering that seemed to bring new life to Alex's eyes. Or was it in her eyes, in the way she was looking at everything?

She felt a little quickening of her heartbeat. The room seemed smaller suddenly and Alex so near. It was almost as if the candle had cast a net out and was pulling them in closer and closer. She was no longer just her but part of this warmth, this radiance that was reaching out and pulling Alex in, too.

Whoa, she'd better be careful. Lemonade and cookies was the intended reward. She stepped back and broke the spell.

"This is so nice," she said brightly. "I've always dreamed of making lemonade by candlelight."

Gracious, was that as inane as it sounded? But she just kept a bright smile on her face and walked around him to the sink...where she found a pump instead of a faucet. A long-handled, old-fashioned pump that people had out as decoration in their garden, not in their kitchen.

"Well, this is another surprise," she said.

Her spirits sagged though as she stared at it. If it wasn't one thing, it was another. But nothing she couldn't handle, she assured herself. And helping Alex was worth putting up with minor little inconveniences. She took the pump handle and worked it up and down. Nothing happened, unless you counted the screeching noise it made.

"Even if you get it to work, that water won't be drinkable," he pointed out.

"Oh, it has to be." A little trickle came out and ran into the sink. It was visible. Was water supposed to be a dark color? "And we can boil it if we need to."

"I doubt that boiling will remove the rust."

"That'll go away the more we pump," she assured him.

But she did pump some more and so did Alex and the water got only slightly better. If she had been making iced tea, the color might not have been noticeable, but it would never do for lemonade. Rats.

Finally Alex stopped pumping and frowned at her. "Don't you think this has gone on long enough?" he said. "This just isn't going to work. We aren't rustic people. We're used to some basic niceties like lights and indoor plumbing."

"Indoor plumbing?" Her stomach really sunk to her toes this time. "What do you mean, indoor plumbing?"

"I mean, the bathroom's an outhouse in back."

For one long horrible second Heather saw a whole parade of snakes and spiders and rabid raccoons lined up outside waiting to attack her. She glanced toward the window over the sink. It was dark outside. Really dark. It wouldn't be snakes and spiders and raccoons, it would be wolves and coyotes and hungry bears. Real fear drained every ounce of energy from her. She could cope with no electricity and with having to pump her water, but an outhouse?

"Look, Heather, enough is enough," Alex said, his voice softer and more persuasive. "It's time to stop this silly game and leave. Get the fuses off Junior." At the mention of his name, Junior started his low growl, but Alex didn't seem to care. "I bet we can find a place to stay in Watton or back in Marquette."

I bet! She shook off her lethargy like a dog shaking off the rain. Nothing was stopping her from helping Alex. Not his attitude. Not her fears. Not even an outhouse.

She looked up at him with a wide grin. "You poor boy," she said, and tucking her arm into his, pulled it close. "We need to show you how to have fun."

"I know how to have fun and this isn't it."

"Don't be such a spoilsport," she teased. "So what if we have no electricity and the bathroom's outside? We can still relax and enjoy ourselves."

"We'd enjoy ourselves more back in civilization."

Geez, he was an old stick-in-the-mud! "Boy, you need to loosen up," she said and slid her arms around him. "Come on, relax."

"Heather, I don't think—"

She tickled him. Not a lot, just a little tweak at his waist. And he jumped! Staid, somber, professorial old Alex was ticklish.

"Heather!" he scolded and tried to move away. "I don't think this is a good idea."

"Why not? Are you afraid to laugh?"

She tickled him again, a little more this time. Her fingers dug into his sides, dancing and pinching and making his squirm. Her hands liked being on him; she liked feeling his muscles tense beneath her touch. She liked the feeling of control, too.

"Heather!" he protested and managed to catch hold of her hands.

"Hey, no fair!" she cried.

But when she looked up to argue, he was closer than she expected. His face was so near to hers and his lips were just begging to be kissed. She forgot all about tickling him and teasing him and making him laugh. She had a sudden craving that only he could satisfy, a sudden urgency that only he could fulfill.

She reached up and met his lips with hers. It was an earth-shattering collision that rocked her very soul. They'd kissed before, but this time her heart was lost. This time there was nothing else in existence but the two of them. This time her whole body exploded into a driving need she'd never felt before.

His arms pulled her closer, tighter, as if there would be no letting go. Which was just what her heart wanted, and just how her arms were holding him. What was this wondrous feeling of lightness and magic that was curling up her insides and turning them to fire? How could this be happening to her?

Alex's lips moved against hers with a persistence that her mouth answered. It was as if there were a hunger in them that was too strong, too raging to be confined to soft and gentle ways. His lips moved again, harder and more demanding. Touch was not enough.

His lips parted and his tongue danced along her lips, teasing and prodding, then sliding inside her mouth. A shiver ran down her spine as raw hunger and desire raced through her. His tongue played with hers, touching her and knowing her in an intimacy that was as scary as it was enthralling.

His hands moved across her back as if they could somehow mold her to him, as if there were ways they could hold each other tighter. Her arms knew the hunger and pulled him close, as she breathed in his scent and the desire-charged air. She could feel his body tremble as her hands ran over his back and his hips. What power she possessed, what magic he gave.

Then suddenly they pulled apart. She didn't know if it was lack of breath or the return of sanity, but they moved slowly away from each other. His eyes mirrored the stunned feel of her heart. Her hands fell from him, his arms let her go, and she took a step back.

"Are you okay?" he asked.

"Of course."

Short of breath certainly, and not too sure what her name was anymore, but who needed air or a name? The kiss's only lacking was that it was too short. It had given her just a fleeting taste of passion, just a teasing glimpse of paradise, leaving her wanting more and more.

"I hadn't planned for that to happen," he said. His voice was stiff and awkward. "Another reason why we shouldn't stay."

She just looked at him, her heart doing flip-flops. There was such a softness in his eyes, such a stunned look of wonder that she knew she had won a small victory. It hadn't been the reward she had planned on, but it had worked nonetheless.

"Even if we wanted to, we couldn't go anywhere tonight," she said. "That road was bad enough in the daylight. It would be impassable at night."

"I'm willing to try."

"I'm not."

He gave her a look, not a happy one, but she couldn't exactly put her finger on what he was thinking. Until he turned to the sink.

"Well, I think I'm going to work on this pump," he said. "See if we can get some decent water."

He was going from kissing her to working on the pump? She just watched as he pumped furiously for a moment, peered at the water coming out, then pumped some more. And after a moment, she understood.

He was retreating, just like Bonnie had that first night. She'd eaten her reward of tuna, then had turned away to give herself a bath. Heather would allow him a little retreat, and would not get discouraged. She'd tamed cats that were far more difficult. She would get through to Alex, too.

Heather's scream woke Alex out of a deep sleep. Grabbing up his gun from under the bag he was using as a pillow, he flew through the bedroom door. She was sitting up in bed, moonlight streaming in the window. No one else was around.

Not quite. A low growl from nearby woke Alex up to reality. Damn.

"What's wrong?" Alex asked on a sigh, slipping the gun into the waist of his jeans. If the dog could growl, he certainly should be able to take care of an intruder. Hell, big as Junior was he should be able to take on an army of intruders.

"I heard someone outside," she said and took a deep breath.

They'd been followed. He thought he'd been watching but obviously not well enough. Senses on edge, he started toward the window, reaching again for his gun.

"They were laughing," she said.

He stopped. "They were laughing?" That didn't make sense.

"Really loud."

Suddenly, it did make sense. He tucked his gun back into his pants and slowly walked over to the edge of the bed. Junior the Monster Dog could—and probably would—rip him to shreds, but he didn't give a damn anymore. He was so tired that all he wanted to do was lie down. He settled for sitting.

"It was a loon," he told her. "A bird. Has a wild call that sounds like laughter."

"That was a bird?" She poked at a little sleeping bundle next to her pillow. "Hey, Bonnie, why didn't you tell me what it was? Aren't cats supposed to know about birds?"

He had no idea what Bonnie's reaction was, because he couldn't take his eyes off Heather. In the pale moonlight, she looked damned delectable sitting there in her cat and dog pajamas. Why couldn't she wear black negligees? Those he could handle. But those damn cat and dog and teddy bear pajamas drove him to the edge.

He put his hands to his head. He was going to have to take a vacation after this assignment was over. No doubt about it.

"I'm sorry I woke you," Heather said.

Alex shook his head. "It's okay."

He hadn't exactly been sleeping anyway. Not since his bed consisted of a rustic plank floor and a blanket that was moth-eaten and stinking from all kinds of little critters having used it for a nest. But he sure wasn't going to mention that to Heather. They'd be back to arguing who got the bedroom and who got the living room.

"Are you sure?" she pressed.

"Positive."

"You know, there's plenty of room for you here," she said, patting the bed next to her.

He stared at her. The moonlight was strong enough to tell him a lot of things, but not nearly bright enough to give him a clue what was in her mind.

"I don't think that's a good idea," he said slowly. "I was fine out in the living room."

"Don't be silly. How can sleeping on that short sofa be preferable to sleeping in a bed?"

Was she just naive and innocent or was she being provocative? Not that it mattered. He wasn't doing anything either way.

"I think the living room is better," he said. "I'm a restless sleeper. I'd keep you awake."

"I'm not sure I'll get back to sleep," she said with

a short laugh. "I think I'll be listening too hard for the laughter that isn't the loon."

He heard the laughter in her voice, but something else was there with it. Worry. Fear. Heather was trying to be brave but she was scared.

He knew that was to his advantage. He knew he should press and poke at her fears until she agreed to leave. But he couldn't.

With a deep sigh, he moved Bonnie into the middle of the bed, laid down himself, then stared up at the ceiling. He felt Junior put his front paws on the foot of the bed, growling as he did so.

"That's okay, Junior," Heather told him. "Everything's fine, boy. Get down."

The dog gave a little whine but he lay back down on the floor. The beast was probably sad because Heather wasn't letting him rip Alex to shreds. And the only reason the dog was obeying was because he figured that he'd get Alex later.

After Junior settled down, Heather did, too. He couldn't quite see her, but he sure could sense her every movement. She was petting Bonnie, her hand moving in a slow, steady motion.

He closed his eyes in agony, a fire ready to engulf him. It didn't matter why Heather asked him to stay here, he would not touch her. He would not think about touching her or kissing her or making hot passionate love to her, even though his body was about ready to scream in agony. He was going to keep her safe. And that meant from everything, including himself.

"So, how do your parents like Arizona?" he asked briskly.

"Fine." Her voice sounded surprised.

"Great." He opened his eyes but kept them on the

ceiling, concentrating on the pale shadows of the trees that the moonlight cast there. He wouldn't notice the soft scent of her perfume wash over him. Okay, he couldn't help but notice it, but he wouldn't react to it. "Climate's great out there."

"Yes. It seems to be."

"Maybe that's where I'll move when I retire." The perfume was like a magnet, drawing him closer and closer. Teasing his senses and testing his willpower. He licked his lips and remembered the taste of her mouth on his. The fire dove deeper into his soul.

"Your retirement's pretty far away," she said.

"I like to plan ahead."

If he liked to plan ahead so damn much, why was he here in this cabin with Heather? Why was he in the same bed as her? Why didn't he have a whole slew of winter thoughts ready to browse through? A blizzard in Siberia. An ice storm in the Yukon. A whiteout in Antarctica.

"I was thinking we could go on a picnic tomorrow," she said.

"Sure." Whatever. Who was the first person to reach the North Pole?

"We'll have to leave Bonnie here of course, but Junior will like exploring with us."

"I bet." He remembered a picture in his history book. Lots of snow blowing around and a frostbitten face staring out of a furred parka. Admiral Perry? Or was it Amundsen?

"I wonder if we'll see many animals around here."

"We might." Okay, who was the first to the South Pole?

"This is such fun," Heather said and yawned. "Gracious. I feel so safe with you here."

"Good." Hell, none of this was working. North Pole. South Pole. You couldn't stop desire by thinking about geography.

He just had to be strong. He could do it. Nothing fazed him. He was coolest under fire.

He heard a soft sound and turned his head. Heather was sleeping. Lying on her side facing him, she had one hand under her pillow and one near Bonnie. She looked so beautiful, so desirable that he thought his heart would burst.

He had to touch her. He had to kiss her. Just the softest of kisses. She would never know. Just the merest brushing of his lips on her hair. Then his fever would go away. Then he could sleep.

Ha. With a mighty effort he rolled onto his side, his back to Heather and Bonnie. He stared at the window with the shadows dancing across the glass.

He wanted to tell her everything. How he wasn't a gambler, how he was just pretending. How he was afraid he had led her into danger. But he couldn't.

The only thing he could do was get her out of here and to safety. That's what he had to concentrate on. Instead of breathing in her perfume, he had to plan on how to get the fuses from Junior. But how was he going to convince Heather to change her mind?

Alex felt a soft movement at his back and for one long moment, his body surged with desire. But then he realized it wasn't Heather, it was Bonnie. The kitten had moved slightly and was leaning against his back as she slept.

Her trust in him was touching. It was—

Of course. It was the answer, that's what it was. He had to act trusting. He had to be a new person, just like Bonnie was a new cat. Then Heather would decide they could go.

Chapter Eleven

"Wouldn't this be a great way to start every day?" Heather asked, sipping at her coffee.

They were sitting out on the steps of the cabin's back porch, looking down a hill at a small lake. The sun was up just high enough to turn the surface of the water to shimmering diamonds. The woods were alive with the sound of birds singing but somehow it seemed like a magical stillness had come over the earth. The air had just a hint of last night's chill. Enough to make her glad to be sitting so close to Alex.

"I thought you'd like having breakfast out here," Alex said.

As usual, he seemed unaffected by her nearness. Her heart was racing and her cheeks felt flush but he was drinking his coffee as calm and relaxed as if he were by himself. But then, he had slept in the same bed as her last night and hadn't so much as touched her. Good thing it didn't matter to her.

"Look, see the deer at the far shore?" Alex said softly.

Heather looked where he was pointing. Sure enough, there were three deer at the water's edge. Watchful. Tense. Ready to flee. They were so beautiful to look at, she could scarcely breathe. Then something startled them and they were gone.

"Wow," Heather said on a sigh.

"Yeah. And here you don't have to worry about them getting hit by a car." He drained his coffee cup and then got to his feet. "Want any more coffee? More toast?"

"I'm fine, thanks."

He went back into the kitchen, leaving her sitting on the step and breathing in the wonderful morning air. Even Junior seemed content to just soak up atmosphere.

Today was a new day. A chance to prove she really wasn't the idiot she must have seemed yesterday. And more time to work on saving Alex. But to do that, she was going to have to stop screaming at bird calls and breaking out in hives at the thought of that outhouse. She could not give Alex a reason to suggest they leave.

She finished her cup and took her dishes back into the kitchen. Alex was washing up the few dishes they'd used.

"The coffee was great," she said and picked up a dish towel. "Guess you got the water running all right."

"Just needed more pumping." Alex said. "My muscles came in handy for something."

Heather felt a now familiar blush wash over her

cheeks. "Where did you learn to cook in such..." Heather looked over at the woodpile by the door, searching for the right word.

"Rustic conditions?"

Heather made a face as she laughed. "I was thinking primitive."

Alex flashed her a broad smile. "Things must have changed a lot since the last time you were here, huh?"

Her laughter died and the faint blush in her cheeks turned to embarrassment. Alex had to know she'd never been up here with Ida Crawford but, in spite of her embarrassment, all she could notice was his smile. Strong. Gentle. Sincere. And what those lips felt like pressed against hers.

Unfortunately that just made her cheeks grow even hotter. She needed to turn her attention to something else. Anything but that smile. Well, not anything. Not his muscular shoulders. Or his deep chest. Or his bulging biceps or chiseled thighs. In fact, his whole body was out of bounds for her thoughts.

"So what would you like to do today?" she asked brightly. It was a risky question, she knew, but maybe it was time to take a chance.

He handed her a cup to dry, a frown on his face. "You have to ask?"

Her heart sank as she dried the cup. He had seemed to be content, enjoying himself even. But she should have known it was too quick.

"If I remember correctly," he said. "I was promised a picnic last night."

She stopped, midway to the pantry, and turned to face him. Those wonderful eyes were dancing with laughter and she had to join in. He wasn't trying to leave!

"A picnic sounds great," she agreed. "But we just had breakfast. I think we need something to do in between."

For a split second, something new burned in his eyes. Just a flickering glimpse of something else. Something that started a fire deep in her soul.

But then he turned back to the dishes. "How about if we pack a lunch and hike down to the lake? I see a canoe down there but I'm not sure what condition it's in."

"A hike would be great." Anything would be wonderful, if she was doing it with Alex. Hiking. Canoeing. Skinny-dipping.

Heavens! Where had that thought come from? She'd never been skinny-dipping and certainly wouldn't here. The bugs would eat her alive.

But the very idea made her cheeks burn and her gaze refuse to go anywhere near Alex. She did wonder, though, if he would find her attractive. She didn't run, but she did do aerobics and watched what she ate. But then, judging from his reactions to her so far, he probably wouldn't even notice if she took her clothes off.

On that depressing note, she hung her dishtowel on the rack. "I'm going to change into better shoes," she said. "Then I'll make us some lunch."

With Bonnie's help, she changed her shoes, then hurried into the kitchen to pack up their lunch. The ice in the cooler was melting, making the menu selection easy. Anything that would spoil when the ice melted was lunch. She left plenty of water and dry food out for Bonnie, then after a quick trip to the outhouse, she met Alex and Junior in back. Her heart was back under control by that time.

"Boy, it's beautiful along here, isn't it?" commented Heather. The pines towered over them, keeping it pleasantly cool, and all around them was the life of the forest. Small flowers dotted the forest floor, even in the densest shade, while in the trees and bushes birds flitted from branch to branch. Their bright colors made them look like flying flowers, escorting them through the forest.

"You forget what nature's really like living back home," Alex said.

Her heart skipped a beat at his words. This was making a difference! The peace here was reaching him. "And we live in a rural area," she added, keeping her voice calm. "Imagine if you lived in the city."

"And wasn't that where we all vowed we were going to live one day?"

She'd never actually wanted to leave Chesterton, though as girls in their Bridal Circle Club they'd discussed it. The big city with all its dangers had intimidated her. But she couldn't say that to Alex without sounding like a scaredy-cat. She was an adventurer this weekend. One who was eager to take on new challenges.

"Boy, this is a big one," Alex said and stopped.

A tree had fallen across the path and its trunk had to be three feet thick. The sheer size of it stopped Heather. She couldn't imagine what would topple such a giant. Or how they would get around it.

The branches were lost in a dense thicket to her right while the base of the trunk must still be partly in the ground for it rose slightly in that direction before it disappeared in the brush. Would they have to go back?

"Give me your hand," he said. "And I'll pull you up."

Was he crazy? This was another of his wild stunts.

Another flirtation with danger. Only this time he wanted her to come along for the ride.

"Heather?" Alex didn't sound impatient, but he did sound confused.

"What about Junior?" Heather asked. "How will he get over?"

"I don't think we need to worry about him," Alex said.

Junior barked as if in agreement, and Heather realized the dog had found his own way over. That only left her.

"Just let me find the best places to put my feet," she told Alex.

"You don't need any," he said. "Just take my hand and you walk up the side while I pull you up."

It sounded so simple. So safe. So why was she fussing? Did she trust Alex or not?

Of course she did.

Reaching up, she took his hand and awkwardly scrambled up the side of the tree. She probably hung on to him too tightly, and most assuredly looked like an idiot while climbing, but she made it to the top in one piece.

"There, that wasn't so bad," he said as he let go of her hand.

"No, it was great," she said, and meant it. She felt exhilarated and alive. And though she was sorry he'd taken his hand away, she had a feeling it had nothing to do with standing up on the tree trunk.

"I think the plan is to jump down on the other side," Alex pointed out gently.

"Oh, right."

He jumped down, joining Junior on the far side of the tree, then reached up for her. But instead of taking her hand this time, he put his hands on either side of her waist and lifted her down.

She had no time to think or ponder or weigh consequences. She had to put her hands on his shoulders to steady herself and once they were there, it was impossible to move them. Just as Alex seemed to be having trouble taking his hands from her waist once he had her on the ground. He just looked down into her eyes and seemed paralyzed.

Well, not totally. He was able to bend his lips to meet hers. And she was able to reach up for that meeting. Their lips touched, their hearts danced, and their bodies clung together in sweet harmony.

But the sweet gentleness only lasted a moment, then hunger took hold. It was as if they were both starving and the other's lips were the only food. As if they were dying of thirst and the other held the blessed drops of water. As if they were suffocating and could only breathe the other's air.

Heather clung to Alex, her arms wrapped around him so tightly, she could feel his heart beating in unison with hers. His lips were the only reality she knew, the only thing that mattered. His hands roamed over her back, pressing her ever closer, his mouth was her lifeline. The only source of her sanity.

One of his hands moved between them, cupping her breast and rubbing the tip with his thumb. Even through her T-shirt and bra, the caress sent her fever soaring, her hunger to know more of his touch grew. She ached to be a part of him, to feel his love all over.

His touch grew hotter, harder, more possessive. Over her breast, then down her side, over her buttock, cupping her, pulling her closer into him. If his touch could set her afire through her clothes, how much hotter would she burn without them?

His lips grew more insistent, as if they were pulling life itself from her. She tightened her arms around him, holding on for all she was worth, but then the world intruded in the form of Junior, nudging them apart.

Heather was lost, stumbling for breath and not even certain where she was. It all came back to her fast enough, but her heart still felt confused.

Alex took a step back from her, his eyes dark and brooding. "I never meant for that to happen," he said.

"Neither did I." She didn't know what else to say. Her heart was still racing, her lips ached for his. It was too hard to think and reason and make polite conversation when her body throbbed with need.

"Maybe we'd better get a move on," he said. "We don't want the mosquitoes to eat us alive."

"We sure don't." Were there even mosquitoes here? She hadn't noticed. "Lead on," she said brightly though.

He gave her a look she chose not to try to read, as he turned to lead the way down the path. She just watched his back as he strode through the tall grass and weeds ahead of her. Ages ago, she'd had a plan but did she even remember it anymore?

Alex glanced back over his shoulder. "You okay?"

"Just peachy."

Something buzzed up near her face and she just batted it away. Her plan hadn't included this attraction, but did that mean it was wrong? She was starting to care an awful lot for Alex, but then didn't she love each and every cat she socialized? It was no different, except of course that she wasn't in love with Alex. She was—

Her feet stopped and she just stared ahead at his rapidly disappearing back. Being alone in the woods was the least of her concerns right now. She couldn't be falling in love with Alex, could she? She would never let herself do something that crazy, would she? That would be even worse than racing across the seawall!

"Heather?" Alex was coming back. "Something wrong?"

"Nope," she said brightly. "Just a stone in my shoe."

Alex strode briskly down the final slope to the lake. Things had gotten a little out of hand there, but nothing to worry about. Nothing that he couldn't keep from happening again. He just had to be careful. He wanted to convince Heather that he was on his way to being cured, nothing else.

He stopped next to the overturned canoe. It looked more weatherworn up close. He didn't have much hope that it would still be watertight, but he turned it over and pulled it closer to the water's edge. Heather caught up with him there and frowned at the canoe. Junior sniffed at its sides as if considering a christening.

"It looks okay," she said.

"You can't really tell until it's in the water," Alex pointed out.

Seeing the extremely small size of the canoe and feeling the heat of her nearness, he was having doubts about this outing anyway. He obviously needed to keep his distance from Heather—something not possible in a small canoe with her. Of course, if things got out of hand out on the water, they would capsize. That would dampen their ardor.

But only until they got to shore. Heather in damp, formfitting clothes would drive any man beyond his limits. Just the thought of her T-shirt clinging to her full breasts made Alex's blood boil with wanting.

"Well, let's put it in the water then," she said and tugged at the prow.

And risk her getting splashed? "I can get it," he cried and pulled the canoe in a slightly different direction. "I don't want you to get wet."

She just laughed, and it was the sound of bells ringing at Christmas. It also doubled his heart rate. The fuses, he had to focus on the fuses, not her laughter.

"I'm not the Wicked Witch of the West, you know."

He was having trouble breathing around her. Following her logic was out of the question. "You're not what?"

"The Wicked Witch of the West," she said. "From *The Wizard of Oz*. You know, she melted when water was thrown on her. Well, I won't melt."

Ah, but he might. Didn't most things melt at high temperatures? "I just didn't see the need for both of us to get splashed," he explained carefully.

"Oh."

While she watched, he dragged the canoe to the edge of the lake and into the water. His feet sunk slightly into the mucky ground as he waded in to get the canoe free of the reeds and cattails. The water rushed around his ankles, then rose up to his knees as he waded farther in. He didn't go in deep enough though. The most throbbing part of his body was still on fire.

"Well?" Heather asked.

Well what? Ah, the canoe. He looked into it. Some

water had seeped in, but not much. "Hard to say," he called out to her. "Maybe we need to let it sit a bit."

"Aw, come on," she pleaded. "Either it's leaking or it's not. I wanted to go on a canoe ride. I've never been in one before."

"You haven't?"

He was torn between giving in to the wistfulness in her voice and keeping a safe distance from her. He had this sudden need to bring a smile to her lips, to give her whatever she wanted. But he knew that wasn't wise. There was something in her smile, in her voice, that could make him forget all about the fuses, but he mustn't let it touch him.

"I really think we need to let it sit," he said.

There was a mooring rope attached to a ring at the bow of the canoe. He took the free end of the rope and waded back to the shore with it.

"We'll just tie it to this tree and check it in an hour," he said as he got out of the water. His shoes squished when he walked—maybe just the thing to quell any romantic thoughts. "Then we can decide."

"I never thought you were this cautious," she said.

"And I never thought you were such a daredevil." He paused for a moment, then looked at the lake and forest around them with a smile. "Gee, it's beautiful around here. Too bad we can't just walk along the shore."

Heather looked around, too, but with a puzzled frown instead of a sad smile. "Why can't we?" she asked.

"Aren't you concerned that Junior might go in the water?"

Heather's frown deepened. "He goes in the water

all the time back home. Toto takes him to the beach on Lake Michigan a couple of times a week.''

''But he's not wearing fuses then,'' Alex pointed out.

A whole array of emotions danced across her face— confusion, surprise, disappointment, then dejection. She looked so absurdly crestfallen that it was all he could to keep his hands at his side. It was all he could do to keep from comforting her, to keep from blurting out that he didn't care about the damn fuses. That she could throw them into the lake for all he cared.

It was a dangerous thought, mostly because it was so appealing. The investigation, his life as a federal agent seemed distant and unreal. Something that he was no longer part of. But it was just his reaction to her eyes. To that kiss back by the fallen tree. To being in the sun too long.

He had to remember that her safety was the most important issue here. And that could only be guaranteed by getting out of here and back to civilization where there were fewer wide-open spaces, fewer unknowns. Where he could arrange for proper protection for Heather.

''I thought you were done trying to get the fuses,'' Heather said.

He held his hands up in a protestation of innocence. ''Hey, I didn't say give them to me. Put them in your pocket. I just didn't want them to get damaged.''

''Oh.'' She glanced over at Junior who was sniffing around at the water's edge. His feet were already as wet as was his face. ''I guess you're right.''

She was giving in, but her voice was so sad, so mournful, that he couldn't even cheer in his heart. He didn't like the fact that only one of them could win, but that was how it was. And that one person had to be him. For her sake.

"Why don't you—"

"Junior," she called out. The dog looked up, tail wagging. "Come on, boy. We can't stay here. Let's go hike in the woods some more."

"Hike in the woods?" His victory disappeared. "I thought—"

"The woods are fine with me," she said brightly. "I haven't been hiking along a lake or in the woods before, so either one's a treat."

She and Junior started back down the trail they'd taken to the lake. She and Junior and the fuses. How did she get so suspicious? Was he losing his touch or was she far more clever all along than he'd suspected?

It was a question that didn't get answered as the day wore on. They hiked through the pine forest, with Heather marveling over the smallest beauties every step. It was like seeing the world all over again, being awakened once more to the wonders of nature.

She delighted in the perfection of a pinecone, and grew excited over the discovery of a tiny pink flower in the shadow of a huge oak. She practically danced along the path in her joy at being there. So what could he and Junior do but laugh along with her? His heart growing heavier and more confused all the while. He needed a distraction.

"So how did you start rescuing cats?" he asked her a few hours later when they'd sat down on a fallen log to eat lunch.

"I'm not sure," she said and pulled some sandwiches and cans of pop out of the backpack he'd been carrying. "It just sort of happened. When I was growing up, I was always finding lost or orphaned animals.

I only brought one home. My mom was sure it was carrying bubonic plague or something. After that, I took them to Penny's farm."

He opened the cans of pop and balanced them on the log between them. "Until you got your own place."

"Yeah, true." Her smile was like a flash of the sun after a storm. "That was the best thing about having a house. I could rescue as many critters as needed rescuing."

He bit into one of the sandwiches as she pulled a collapsible water dish for Junior and a bottle of water from the backpack. She set the dish up on the ground and filled it with water for the dog who lapped it up gratefully.

Alex put his sandwich down slowly. She'd not only thought about lunch for them, she'd thought about Junior, too. She had to be the kindest, most genuinely good person he'd ever met. Which made it all the more necessary to get her out of here and out of the mess he was involved in.

Heather sat back down on the log and picked up her sandwich. "I have a question for you," she said.

"Why do I gamble?" he guessed, and was overcome with the need to tell her the truth. He couldn't, he knew that. And wouldn't. But still he hated the deception more than he expected. "I just like the thrill, I guess. But I really don't gamble as much you think."

Oh, no? Wasn't this whole weekend a gamble in a way? But not in the way she meant.

She took a bite of her sandwich and frowned at him. "If you don't gamble much, why did you get beaten up?"

"I didn't," he protested. "I fell and hit my head on your sprinkler."

"Then why did you get a threatening phone call?"

"I didn't—" He stopped, his eyes narrowing. "What call?"

Her cheeks blushed but he was no longer in the mood to be charmed. "Someone called when I went over to close your door," she admitted.

"Someone called?" he snapped. Junior stopped drinking and turned his head toward Alex with that low growl deep in his throat, but Alex didn't care. "Why didn't you tell me?

"Be quiet, Junior." She turned back to Alex. "What was there to tell? They called to tell you that you'd get beaten up last night if you didn't pay them."

Damn! The operation was racing ahead and he wasn't there to point it in the right direction. "You had no right to keep that from me," he said.

"Why? So you could stay there and be all macho while they pounded the hell out of you? I don't think so."

"Maybe I was going to pay them."

"Yeah, right," she said with a short laugh. "Like you were about to pay them when you fell on my sprinkler."

He took a deep breath to try to hold in the anger. It didn't work so he tried another. It was less successful than the first. What was that he'd thought earlier about how good and kind she was? Well, he'd been wrong. She was a meddler. A busybody of the highest level.

"None of this was your affair," he said stiffly. "I was handling it just fine myself."

She put her half-eaten sandwich down and took his

hand. "Alex, be honest. You can't handle this. You need to go to the police and tell them all about it."

He didn't like his hand in hers. Somehow it pulled the anger from him, and he needed it to stay strong. "All about what?" he said. "They don't care if I place a few bets."

"But they would care about those people threatening you. Let them help you."

He stopped, torn and conflicted. She'd opened a path before him. To take it would mean he was a heel, a crud, an absolute worm. But to not take it would be even worse—it would mean keeping her in the potential danger of the unsecure cabin. He had no choice.

"You're right," he said slowly. "I got in over my head and need to go to the authorities. It's the only way out of this mess."

Her eyes were so gentle and understanding, so sympathetic. "It'll be hard to admit it all, but it's the only way to really put it behind you."

"And maybe in stopping them, it'll keep someone else from getting pulled into their claws."

Heather got to her feet. "I hadn't thought of that," she cried. "Of course, it's not just you who was in danger but others, too. We should get you back to Chesterton. Toto'll know what to do."

She seemed ready to march out on a Crusade. "I think we can finish lunch first," he said.

She looked at the sandwich lying there and laughed as she sat back down. "Yeah, I guess we can stay a few minutes longer."

"Or even a few hours," he said. "You haven't had your canoe ride."

She just waved off his words. "Oh, that doesn't matter. I can have a canoe ride anytime."

"You said you haven't managed one yet so, if the canoe is seaworthy, we're going canoeing."

A few hours one way or another was hardly going to matter. And this way he could give her her canoe ride. It was the least this heel, this worm, this scum of the earth could do for her.

They glided over the water like in a dream, slipping along the edges of the forest silently. The only sound was Junior's breathing and the slight splashing of Alex's paddle in the water. Up ahead of him in the canoe, Heather sat still, just gazing into the trees as they passed, catching quick glimpses of deer and maybe even a fox.

"This is just so beautiful," Heather said softly. "I can't believe it."

Even though his heart weighed a ton, he couldn't help but smile at her. Her pleasure was so pure. "And you were willing to miss it. Aren't you glad I insisted?"

She looked over her shoulder, around Junior who was sitting in the middle of the canoe, and made a face at Alex. "Yes, you were right."

They glided past the deer feeding at the water's edge and the forest grew denser. Rather than peer in under the trees, she oohed and aahed over the fish darting up to snatch bugs off the surface of the water. The turtles sunning on fallen logs. And the family of ducks sitting in the shade under an overhanging branch. He had seen all this before, but he felt her excitement and it seemed new to him, too. Though his eyes did seem to stay on her more than the wildlife around them.

"I never knew canoeing could be this great," she said. "I should have been doing it for years."

''Well, it helps to have a great place to canoe,'' he pointed out. ''I don't think you'd see all this wildlife along Lake Palomara.''

Two dragonflies landed on the surface of the water next to them, their wings catching the sun and shining in iridescent splendor. ''Oh, look!'' Heather cried. ''Aren't they beautiful?''

Alex just laughed. ''What was in your lunch?'' he teased. ''Those are bugs. You know, those things I thought you were afraid of.''

But she just held on to the sides of the canoe as they skimmed over the water. ''Me, afraid? I don't think so.'' A submerged branch scraped the bottom of the canoe and she laughed even as she shivered. ''I feel too wonderful to be afraid of anything. I am so happy that you're going to ask Toto for help.''

The atmosphere suddenly changed. A cloud passed over the sun, even though it was perfectly clear. Damn. It shouldn't mean that much to her.

She looked over her shoulder at him as if sensing his change of mood. ''Stop looking so glum,'' she told him. ''It's all going to work out fine.''

Nothing was going to work out fine, not like she thought. The knowledge nagged at him. ''When do you stop worrying about others and take care of yourself?'' he snapped. ''You shouldn't be basing your happiness on what I do.''

''Why not? You're a friend and I care about you.''

''You should worry more about yourself.''

''I do worry about myself when I need to,'' she countered. ''But right now we need to get you safe.''

Her good-heartedness was like an annoying fly that wouldn't leave him alone. ''How do you know I meant anything I said," he asked her. "Maybe I made it all up just to get the fuses."

But she just laughed. "I know you, Alex Waterstone. And I trust you. You wouldn't lie about all this to me. I know you wouldn't."

Her certainty was like a knife slicing into him, slicing and turning and digging in deeper. He wouldn't lie? Everything he'd done since he came back to Chesterton had been a lie. Everything he'd said to her since he found her in his yard trying to catch Bonnie had been a lie. Damn. His whole life was one big lie. How had he thought he could have a quiet peaceful last hour with her? Another hour of his lies?

"I think we'd better turn back," he said.

"Does it matter which fuse goes where?" Heather asked, leaning in the open car door. The late afternoon sun was coming through the trees at just the wrong angle and she could hardly see Alex. "I didn't mark which came from where."

Alex was lying across the car seats so he could get at the fuse box under the dashboard. "The different sizes go in different slots," he said. "Hopefully there's a schematic in here."

Heather bit her lip, waiting as he pulled the cover off the box. He seemed pretty patient though. Almost gentle with her. Maybe he saw a light at the end of his tunnel now and was more relaxed.

"Yeah, there's one here," he said. "It'll take a little figuring out, but it'll be fine."

She sighed in relief. "That's good. I hadn't really wanted to strand us here permanently."

"I'm glad to hear it."

"I guess I could start packing up our stuff."

She hated to leave his side, silly as it seemed. It wasn't like she thought he was going to run out on her or anything. Or that he was going to change his mind. It was just some strange sense of sadness that everything was going to be different soon. As much as she wanted him to see the danger in the life he led, she was sorry realization had come so quickly. She wouldn't have minded spending another day or two here. But that was being silly.

"Junior and I are going inside," she said. "Call if you need anything."

She wandered into the kitchen. With a sigh, she patted Junior's head. "Guess we'd better tell Bonnie it's time to go home."

She stopped patting him and frowned as she looked around. Funny, the little kitten was usually around someplace. She wasn't terribly confident yet and didn't rush up to greet Heather like her other cats did, but she wasn't so standoffish, either. Worry dried up her mouth.

"Where's Bonnie?" she asked Junior.

The dog just looked at her, wagging his tail.

"Come on, Junior. Find Bonnie. Go get Bonnie."

The dog turned this time and trotted through the cabin. Heather followed on his heels, her stomach knotting itself up. The kitten had to be here someplace. She probably was asleep and hadn't heard them come in. Junior stopped at the bed, then hopped up, looking proud of himself.

"Is she here?" Heather asked, and looked under the pillows.

Nope.

She pulled back the quilt even though it looked smooth and flat.

Nope. No Bonnie.

She got on her hands and knees and looked under the bed. When she saw nothing that way, she slid under the bed, but the bottom of the mattress was solid. There was no place for the kitten to hide. Where could she be?

Alex came in while she was searching the living room. "I got them all back in," he announced, then stopped. "What's the matter?"

Heather clutched at the back of the chair for support. "I can't find Bonnie anyplace."

"You can't find her? She's got to be here someplace."

Heather took a deep breath. "I've been looking and she's just not here." Suddenly she was close to tears. "What if she got outside? She wouldn't survive more than a few hours out there at most. She's just a baby."

Alex was at her side, leading her over to the sofa. She just buried her face in his chest, so afraid she could barely think.

"What am I going to do?" she asked, fighting back tears. "I can't leave without her."

"Who said anything about leaving?" Alex snapped. "If we have to stay all month to find her, we will."

All month! But Heather wiped at her eyes and wiped that scary notion away. They would find her and find her soon.

But the kitten wasn't in the pantry, or under the living room sofa, under the table or in the fireplace. She wasn't on the bookshelves or behind the pillows on the armchair.

"Maybe we'd better check outside while it's still light," Alex said slowly.

Heather nodded, biting back her worst fears. She

should have listened to Alex and left Bonnie at home. A setback in her socialization was nothing compared to losing her.

Alex, Heather and Junior circled the house, calling for Bonnie and peering under bushes. They widened their circle, then went individually, but there was no sign of her. The shadows grew longer and deeper; finding her in the dark would be almost impossible.

"We'll get the lantern from the pantry and light that," Alex said. "Maybe if she sees the light, she'll come home."

They trudged into the house. Even Alex's steps were slow and heavy, Heather noticed. He was feeling discouraged too.

"Maybe we should take her carrier out with us," Heather suggested. "She likes to sleep in it."

Heather stopped and stared at Alex. "Did you…"

He shook his head. "You?"

She shook hers, then they both practically ran across the living room to the cat carrier in the corner. Heather picked it up and nodded with a grin. She slowly turned the opening toward the light and they peeked inside. Bonnie lay curled up in the back, sound asleep. Heather put the carrier down softly.

"You mean the little dickens has been in there all along?" he whispered. Then he started to laugh and pulled Heather into his arms. "I take it she had a hard day and was busy sleeping it off."

"Hey, you can't expect a girl to forgo her beauty sleep just to answer roll call."

"Silly me."

Silly Heather. She'd forgotten how hard it was to breathe while in his arms. And then coupled with the relief over finding Bonnie, she could barely stand.

Alex must have felt her wobbliness for he looked down at her. His lips were so temptingly close, but he used them to frown instead of to revive her.

"You okay?" he asked.

"Sure," she said with a laugh. "Just a little weak with relief."

He helped her to the sofa and sat her down. That was all well and good, but then he stood up. She preferred his arms closer to her.

"You just sit here," he said. "I'll make us some dinner."

"I'm okay," she insisted and got to her feet. "I thought we were going to leave."

He gently pushed her back down on the sofa. "What's a few hours?" he said. "You just relax. And don't take your eyes off of our hide-and-go-seek champ."

Our? It was just a casual use of the word. It meant nothing but her heart still skipped a beat. "Did you hear that, Bonnie?" she whispered as she slipped the cat out of the carrier. "Maybe we don't want to rush home after all."

Rushing did not seem to be in anybody's plans. Alex made a simple salad with all the fresh fruits and vegetables that were left, and then heated up a can of soup to go with it. It didn't take long to make, and didn't have to take long to eat, but they both just lingered over it. Then rather than clean up and leave, they went out back to sit on the steps and watch the sun sink slowly in the west while Junior snoozed in the last warming rays of the day.

"Shouldn't we be going?" she finally asked, though she would have been content to stay there for hours.

Alex pulled Heather into his arms. "When we

couldn't find Bonnie, my perspective changed. I'm not in quite such a rush to go back to the way things were.''

"Oh.''

She was not going to argue, not nestled in his arms as nicely as she was. She was thinking, though, that they were other things they could be doing so close together like this.

"Do you think—'' she began.

"Want to—'' he said at the same time.

They were laughing for only a moment before she looked up at him while he was looking down at her and the earth stopped. It was such a short distance between their lips, and one so speedily traversed.

His mouth took hers with the hunger of ages and she answered back in kind. Need, yearning, desire, longing. All merged in the touch of their lips against the other's. There was a desperation in his touch, which puzzled and saddened her. Why should kissing her bring on sadness?

But the very thought made her bolder and more daring. Her lips moved against his, as if she could pull the sadness from his soul. As if she could wrest the demon from him that was trying to cast a shadow on their joy.

Her arms wound around his neck, pulling him closer to her body, closer to her heart. If she could just get him close enough, she could make him forget the clouds that wanted to block their sunshine. She could make him feel the warmth inside her.

But then he was releasing her and there was nothing she could do but let go also. The sadness was still in his eyes, farther back and harder to see, but she knew it hadn't disappeared. There was a hint of it in the way his hands slid down her arms to take her hands in his. There was a trace of it in his soft laughter, and a whisper of it in the sweetness of his smile.

"You're a dangerous woman, Heather Mahoney," he said with a short laugh. "You look so quiet and calm, but underneath there's a tiger ready to chew me up."

Heather just laughed. A tiger inside her? Hardly. "It's got to be the stinging nettle," she said and got to her feet. "Either that or you're possessed."

"There is that possibility."

His voice was soft, almost as if he were talking to himself, so she chose not to answer. She reached her hand down for his.

"Come on," she said. "We need to get packed."

He got up by himself but didn't relinquish her hand, keeping it snuggly in his. "You're right. It's going to be dark soon."

"And we still have dishes to do. Come on, Junior," Heather called and then they followed the dog inside.

It was just as well that that spell had been broken, Heather thought as she started cleaning up the dinner dishes. She was here to help Alex break free of his dependence on gambling, not get herself involved. Her life was complicated enough already, thank you.

"Did you ever have a time when nothing seems simple and straightforward?" Alex asked.

She laughed and rinsed out the bowls. "Have I ever had a time when it did?"

"No, I'm serious," he said.

She looked at him then; his eyes were wearing a troubled look as he sat on the edge of the table. Something was bothering him. She put the bowl down and leaned her back against the sink.

"Actually, so was I," she said. "Nothing has ever been simple and straightforward as long as I can remember. Everything has a million possible consequences and all of them dire."

"So how do you decide on a course of action?"

"Toss a coin. Pick the squeakiest wheel. Go through the closest door."

He stood up, walking ever so slowly across the kitchen toward her. There was something in his walk, something in his eyes, something in the fire that seemed to race before him to scorch her before he was even within reach. He stopped, just a bare few inches from her, and put a hand on the counter on either side of her.

"What if what you want is purely for the moment with no possibility of a tomorrow?"

She just stared up into his eyes, stared at those lips that had the power to drive her wild, stared at the fact that tonight might be the only night they would ever have. But she was thirty-three years old and tired of playing it safe. Tired of backing away from passion. Did pleasure have to come with a guarantee?

She reached up and touched his lips with a gentle caress, followed by a whisper-soft touch of her lips. She felt his heat radiating into her heart, felt his hungers and his iron-tight self-control.

"I think it's getting too dark to drive that road," she said, her voice a mere breath on the air. "We could regret trying to."

Her caught her hand in his and brought those fingers back to his lips, touching each one in a heart-tingling kiss. "We could regret staying."

"We could regret not."

She took her hand back and slid it behind his head,

pulling his lips down to hers. Their mouths met with a jolt of electricity, with a spark that set fire to their hearts. It was all the magic she'd ever dreamed of, all the wonder that she had longed for.

They kissed and kissed and kissed again, until their hearts were racing too fast to think or question or even breathe. There was nothing but their needs, their lips, their hungry bodies. His touch ignited her soul into a wonderful fiery ball of cravings. She'd never felt like this before, never felt needs controlling her body and driving her actions.

Alex's mouth left hers, trailing kisses along her cheek and neck, sparking her hunger into an even greater intensity. Then she felt him bury his face in her hair, breathing soft kisses into it.

"I love how you smell," he said, his voice as unsteady as her knees felt. "It's like springtime. Like everything coming to life again."

It was how she felt, strangely enough. How his touch made her feel. As if she'd been asleep forever and was only coming awake, alive, with his caress. She moved deeper into his arms, wanting only the feelings to continue.

But he moved away from her slightly. "If we're going to go, we'd better do it now," he murmured.

"While there's still light?"

"While there's still sanity."

But she was through with that. For just this night, she was going to live for the moment and treasure the now. This was all she wanted and in the morning, she would worry about tomorrow and all the days after that.

"I think the only place we should go is in the bedroom," she said softly.

"I think there's light enough left for that," he returned and swooped her up in his arms.

The last lingering glow of the sunset lit the way through the cabin to the bedroom and he laid her gently on the bed. Heather didn't know if it was the dying glimmers of the daylight or the fiery passion that they were feeling, but the room seemed filled with a rosy hue. A golden glow as if they were flying in the heavens.

Alex kicked off his shoes, and reached over to pull hers off. Her bare feet against the quilt was sensuous enough, but when his hands roamed slowly over them, she thought she would start purring with pleasure. But then his caress moved upward and his hands slid under her shirt. His touch was cool against her heated skin, that grew ever hotter from his touch.

He tugged at her shirt and pulled it over her head, then loosened her bra. If she'd had thought left or time to be embarrassed she might have wondered if her body was pleasing to him, but he gave her no chance. Bending down, he took the tip of one breast in his mouth and let his tongue tease it. He sucked on it, and closed his lips around it, pulling and tugging and causing hot surges of desire to race through her.

She moaned softly, and then again as his mouth took the other breast captive. Wrapping her hands around him, holding him as close as possible, she let him take her on a ride into the sky. She'd never felt like this, never had this sweet knot of tension building inside her before.

She clung to him, wondering how love could get any more wonderful, when his hand slid over her stomach. Shivers of awe and delight raced through her, then his caress went lower. Under her shorts, under her panties, his hand found the core of her womanhood. A touch, another, soft and gentle, even and steady. She felt the knot of tension grow and grow as her heart pounded.

So this was love. So this was the magic that awakened only in special arms. But she wanted to feel her hands bringing that explosive power to him.

She pushed him over, and pulled at his shirt, tugging it over his head. "Tell me what you like," she whispered. "Tell me what to do for you."

"Anything." His voice was raw and ragged, a hoarse echo of its normal self. "Everything."

She ran her hands over his chest, through his chest hairs, until she could feel his body tremble. She leaned over to lick at his nipples and felt him quiver beneath her. Her hands roamed over his stomach, wondering at how good it all felt. How right. How necessary.

Then he took her hand and pulled it down lower, down to the center of his manhood. She touched, a little afraid, a little bold, but mostly in a hot feverish need. Her fingers ran over his hardness; each stroke seemed to be an agony of pleasure for him.

In a moment, though, he seemed to have reached some peak for he pushed her back and pulled her shorts and panties off. With the same urgency, she tugged at his until they lay naked in each others's arms. Hot burning hungers between.

She spread her legs and he slid inside her. There was exquisite pain for a moment, then exquisite pleasure. He moved against her, with her, in her, to a steady rhythm even as he showered her face in kisses. Even as he clung to her as if they were the only two people in existence.

His body did magical things to hers. She felt alive and on fire and ready to explode. Her joy seemed to dance in the air, to fly on the clouds and soar within the boundaries of his arms. No, it was heaven they were reaching. A showerburst of stars as she clung so tightly to him that she thought they would be forever one. And then there was a sweet soft falling sensation.

They clung even tighter, then lay in each other's arms. She smiled at him, suddenly feeling almost shy.

"Wow," she said. "What do you do for an encore?"

He started to laugh as he pulled her closer. His lips lightly took hers. "Make that a double wow," he said. "Lady, you are really something."

She just closed her eyes and cuddled into the shelter of his arm where she would always be safe.

Chapter Twelve

Heather snuggled down under the sheet, hiding her face against Alex's body and trying to stay asleep in the semilight of a rainy morning. She heard the rain beating against the cabin roof, and heard the crash of thunder, but was too comfortable to care. This was a morning to loll about in bed. Last night had been so perfect. She had loved and been loved, and it had been wonderful.

The wind was picking up, blowing so hard that it was almost whistling. She supposed she ought to look outside—if she moved just a fraction she could look out the open window—to make sure there wasn't a tornado coming, but that would mean moving away from Alex's side. Away from her blissful cocoon.

Junior started to growl and she knew she was going to have to wake up. Of course, that might not be a bad

idea, come to think of it. It might present more satisfying ways of reliving last—

"Damn!" Alex exploded, flinging himself out of
bed.

Heather was awake at that and sitting up. The whining, whistly noise of the wind was still there. She could
hear it over the storm, Junior's barking and Alex's
swearing, but it didn't quite sound like the wind anymore.

"Alex?"

He turned to look at her, his eyes blazing angry—
but not at her, she sensed. "You'd better get dressed,"
he said and grabbed his jeans.

"Get dressed?" She sat up in bed. "What is that
noise?"

But Alex didn't reply. He'd gotten his jeans and shirt
on, and was tossing her clothes onto the bed. "Come
on, Heather. Put your clothes on."

She reached for her T-shirt and pulled it on as a loud
crash of thunder shook the cabin. She shivered, her fear
of storms suddenly rushing back. This was a terrible
one, and a very real sense of impending danger took
hold of her. Alex was going over to the side window,
where Junior was in a frenzy with his barking. She had
to get them away from there. That's where the danger
was.

"Alex, come away from there," she called out. "Junior, here, boy. Here."

Neither of them seemed to notice she had spoken.
Her stomach was turning upside down and inside out.
She got out of bed and pulled on her shorts, only then
realizing she'd forgotten her bra and underpants. She
shoved them under the pillow.

"Alex? What is going on?"

But it wasn't his voice or the storm she heard.

"This is the police." The bellowing voice from outside echoed through the cabin. "Come out immediately with your hands above your heads and no one will get hurt."

Junior was straining at the window, barking and leaping, but all Heather could do was stare at Alex, her heart pounding so it was drowning out all the other noise. Police? "Alex, what is going on?"

He turned from the window then, a look of defeat in his eyes. "Will you get Junior calmed down? I don't want anyone to get hurt." His voice held no emotion. Nothing but words.

Heather just kept on staring at him, her heart slowing down as she forced herself to not fall apart. She knew what had happened—the bad guys had found them and were pretending they were the police.

She had to pull herself together. Alex needed her help. "Junior, quiet." The dog quit barking and she turned to Alex. "All right. We need a plan."

But Alex was wearing defeat heavily around his shoulders. "You need to put some shoes on," he said. "And then we need to go outside."

Didn't he understand? She would help him fight. "No, no. If we go outside, they'll get us."

"If we don't go outside, they're going to fill this place with tear gas."

"Tear gas?" She slipped on her athletic shoes. "That's ridiculous. They only do that in movies and then it's the police who do that."

"Those are the police out there," Alex replied.

"This is your last warning." The amplified voice must have been audible for miles. "Come out with your hands up or we're coming in."

She stopped tying her shoes and stared at him, her eyes looking into his. This was more complicated than she had thought.

"What are the police doing here?" Her words came out in a hoarse whisper.

"They want to rescue me."

Rescue him? She started, as a clap of thunder shook the cabin. If only she was still asleep and dreaming all this! But the awful ache in her stomach kept reminding her she was awake. "Rescue you? From what?"

A crooked grin slowly stretched out his lips. "I think from you."

"Me?"

But he didn't explain any more. He just leaned over and kissed her forehead. Softly. Tenderly. In goodbye. His hand lightly brushed her cheek. His eyes were filled with the memories of last night for a long moment, then they turned shuttered and empty.

What in the world was he doing? But she couldn't ask. Her eyes had filled with tears and somehow they were choking her, cutting off her ability to speak. She had nothing to say anyway.

Alex went to the bedroom door, then paused. "This whole thing is just a bad misunderstanding. I'm going outside to talk to them. Come out in a few minutes, but make sure Junior stays cool."

Heather could barely hear his footsteps over the rain as he went across the living room and into the kitchen. When she heard the back door close, she sank onto the bed. Her legs just wouldn't hold her up anymore.

What in the world was going on? Why would the police be coming up here for Alex?

She got to her feet and went over to the window.

The yard, dreary-looking in the downpour, was the parking place of a half dozen police cars.

Among the cars were groups of men and women, all wearing dark waterproof blue jackets with FBI in large letters on the back. They were indeed police. As she watched, Alex walked through the rain toward them, then he was surrounded and lost from her sight.

She blinked back tears. Oh, Lord. They were going to arrest Alex.

Oh, heavens. She couldn't let that happen. She loved him. He needed her. Whatever he had done was a mistake; he hadn't meant to. It was because his father died and he'd missed him so.

Terrible fear eating at her heart, Heather raced through the cabin and rushed out into the rain. The thunder rolling through the forest was almost deafening, but she didn't care. Alex needed her.

"Officers," she yelled as she raced toward the group that seemed to be in charge. "Officers, I can—"

She stopped. Alex was about ten feet away. He wasn't handcuffed. He didn't even appear threatened in any way. An uneasy feeling began to dance in the pit of her stomach. Maybe it was the fact that everyone had turned to stare at her.

"So this is the neighbor," another man said.

Heather turned to face him. She had no idea what he was talking about, but her mother had always taught her to address the person who addressed you.

"Sir." She shivered even though the drenching rain was warm. "There has to be some mistake. Alex is a good and decent man. You can't arrest him."

"Heather—" Alex began.

But she didn't look his way. If she looked into his deep-brown eyes, she would be lost. She'd never be able to fight for him. She'd start to cry and look like a fool and no one would listen to her.

"Maybe he made a mistake," she continued, the rain plastering her hair to her face. She squinted away the water. "But that's all it was. A mistake. He didn't mean any harm. He's gentle and kind and caring. He even helped me catch a feral kitten. You can't arrest him."

"Arrest him?" The other man was frowning. "I don't see anything I can arrest him for."

A little ray of hope took hold of her heart. She wiped the wet from her face, not certain if it was tears or rain. "You don't?"

"No." The man looked over at Alex. "But I certainly see a lot I can reprimand him for."

"Reprimand?" It was an odd word to use, and Heather just stared at the man. She shivered again as a certain stillness took over her heart. "I don't understand."

"Alex is an experienced agent," the man stated. "He should have known better than to lead us on this wild-goose chase."

"Experienced agent?"

That stillness crept out from her heart, freezing her hands, her feet, her brain. She felt as dense as a piece of wood. Fear. Dread. Horror. They were all paralyzing her, keeping her from connecting the dots and making sense of all this.

"What—" she began, then stopped.

The man she'd been talking to seemed to have forgotten her and was busy with Alex and another man. She knew Alex was looking her way, but she refused to meet his eyes. Somehow she couldn't yet. Somehow it would make everything all clear and all wrong.

Bits of the men's conversation began to penetrate. Miss another payment. Set up a meet. Talk about influence. Placing bets. Fixing games. It was enough to make her head swim. But it was also enough to make everything very very clear.

This whole thing—everything, even his professorship!—had been a game. Nothing was real or right or true. Nothing.

"Come on," Casio said. "Get in the car. We're going to drown if we stand out here any longer."

Alex clenched his jaw, his eyes following Heather back into the house. She had looked so beaten down, and it wasn't just being soaked by the rain. "Just a minute. I need to talk to Heather."

"You don't need to do anything," Casio snapped. "Everything's taken care of. Willa is driving the woman and the dog back."

"She has a cat, too."

Casio shrugged. "I'm sure Willa can handle it. We need to get to Chicago. This thing is about to bust wide-open."

Alex just looked at Casio. He knew that he had to go, knew that they were at a crucial point in the investigation. But he wasn't leaving until he'd seen Heather. "I need to talk to her. I need to make sure she's all right."

He didn't wait for permission, but strode through the muddy yard and back into the house. It was silent inside, except for the sound of Junior's feet on the wooden floor.

"Hi, boy," Alex said softly. "Where's Heather?"

For once the dog didn't growl at him, but looked

nervously over toward the bedroom. Alex nodded and patted the dog's head.

"Okay, thanks."

He walked softly over to the bedroom door, his heart made of concrete and dragging him down. He had no idea what he'd say to her, no idea what he ought to say. What would ease her pain?

He stopped in the doorway, thrown from his thoughts by the sight of Heather lying on the floor, half under the bed.

"Heather?" he cried.

"Go away," she said, her voice muffled by the bed. "You and your noise have scared Bonnie enough already. Just leave us alone, will you?"

He stood next to her, trying to keep from seeing the bed and all its memories. "Heather, I don't have much time."

"Come on, Bonnie honey," she cooed from under the bed. "Everything's all right. I made the bad men go away."

Was he one of the bad men? No reason to ask. He was the worst.

"Heather," he said softly. "I'm really sorry you had to find out like this."

She came out from under the bed, holding Bonnie in one hand. "That's probably the only true thing you've said to me in the past twelve months. I'm sure you'd have liked it much better if I'd never found out."

He tried not to wince. "That came out wrong."

"I'm sure it did."

She looked so small and fragile, so hurt. But she refused to look at him, refused to give him any ground for his apology. Not that he deserved any.

He watched as she sat on the bed, cuddling Bonnie. Memories of last night came rushing back, too strong, too powerful for him to even breathe for a moment. Finally he was able to think again.

"I wanted to tell you the truth," he said. "I hated the deception."

"So you let me make a fool of myself."

"You were trying to help me," he said. "Nothing you did was foolish."

She looked up at him. "Nothing? Everything was!" She stopped and seemed to settle herself. "But it's partly my fault. I should have known you weren't a gambler. Especially not a bad one."

He pulled back a bit, her words making him slightly defensive. "How should you have known?" he asked.

She just gave him a look and went back to cuddling Bonnie. "First of all, you aren't the gambling type; it's not dangerous enough. And then, I can't see you losing, not big time."

He wasn't sure he liked her easy analysis of him. "People lose big all the time."

"Yeah, people who take the same risk over and over again. Once you raced across the seawall, you went on to other thrills."

He frowned. He wasn't that easy to read. He couldn't be. "That was years ago," he pointed out. "I have grown up, you know."

"But you haven't changed." She got to her feet. "The danger still gives you a rush. In fact, that's probably why you let me stupidly hang around, trying to help you. It was another thrill. How far could you go before I found out?"

"It wasn't like that all," he snapped.

"Oh, give me a break," she cried. "You could have stopped this at any time, and you didn't."

"I tried," he said tersely. "A number of times. But you were so hell-bent on rescuing me that you wouldn't listen."

Her eyes flashed with anger. "I see. It was all my fault."

"Partly, yes." Suddenly he saw the truth spread out before him and he couldn't deny it any longer, painful as it was. "You'd rescued lots of cats before. Been there, done that. But here was a person to rescue. A poor needy slob who just fell into your lap and you couldn't resist."

"You can't believe that," she said.

He didn't know what he believed anymore. Her suspicions of him still hurt, ached, nagged at him like an open wound. If she could think the worst of him, maybe it was because she'd never seen him as a person in his own right. And that was what hurt most of all, for some crazy reason.

"Why can't I believe it?" he snapped. "Why else would you have done all this?"

She just looked at him, the anger slipping from her eyes and a bleakness settling in its place. She opened her mouth as if to speak, but no words came out. He waited, for what he had no idea. But then after an eternity, she turned away.

"Come on, little Bon-Bon," Heather said hoarsely to the kitten in her arms. "We're going to go home now."

He waited just a moment for her to turn, to respond, to say something to him that would make the terrible pain leave his heart. But she just buried her face in the kitten's fur as she carried her to the cat carrier in the corner.

What had he expected? What had he wanted? He grabbed his duffel bag from the corner, and quickly turned, hurrying out of the room. Junior was waiting at the door, and Alex stopped.

"You take care of her," Alex told him. "Make sure she stays safe."

The dog wagged his tail, accepting the responsibility. And would probably do a better job than Alex had. With that thought sticking in his throat, he hurried back outside.

The rain had stopped, and he was almost sorry. There was something about the rain that fit his mood. A good dark, rip-roaring thunderstorm was what he wanted right now. Instead, the sun was starting to peek through the clouds. Damn.

Casio straightened up from where he was leaning against a car. "You ready now?"

"As ready as I'll ever be." Alex went around and got in the driver's seat, slamming the door good and hard. "But I'm driving."

"Whatever," Casio said and got in the other side. "We've got a chopper waiting in Marquette. You should be back in Chicago by early afternoon."

"Great." Alex turned the motor on and peeled out, ignoring the mud that tried to slow him down. "I can't wait to get back on the case."

"The Chesterton exit is up next," Heather said.

"Oh. You're awake," Willa said. "That's good. I was wondering how I'd find your house."

Heather just smiled at the agent, but said nothing. Actually, she'd been awake for a while and watching out the window as the car sped down the highway. It had just seemed easier to pretend that she was napping. Or was it safer?

She glanced into the back seat. Bonnie was sleeping in her carrier and Junior was looking out the window intently. No one seemed too disturbed by the events of the morning. No one but her, that is. Her heart felt as if it had turned to stone, except stone didn't usually hurt so much. Good thing she hadn't fallen in love with Alex. Just think of how it would hurt then!

She turned back to Willa. "It was nice of you to drive home with me. It's a long drive by yourself."

"No problem," the agent said. "It was a nice break, believe me."

"Are you involved in this investigation with Alex?"

"Me? No, I'm just a field agent assigned to this area. Actually, none of us knew quite what was going on. Just that Waterstone was missing and had been heading up to that area. After some agents talked to the owner of the grocery store in Watton, we were all sent up there to surround the cabin."

"So you were expecting some bad guys or something?"

"Yeah, until Alex came out and explained."

Heather stared straight ahead, feeling as if she were facing a firing squad. "Turn right up at the light," she said and took a deep breath. "And what did he tell you all?"

Willa slowed the car and turned before she spoke. "Not much of anything. He really laid into his supervisor, though. Said he had everything under control. That you'd had car trouble and were going to leave in the morning."

Heather said nothing, but turned to look out the window as tears filled her eyes. What had she expected? That he'd say he'd fallen in love with her and had treasured every moment they were together? She should be glad he didn't say that she'd kidnapped him and kept him from leaving.

"Right at the stoplight," she said, her voice thick and hoarse from holding back the tears. "Then right at the next light."

Willa gave her a look, Heather could feel it, but the woman said nothing for which Heather would be forever grateful. It was bad enough that she was an idiot; she didn't have to let everyone know. In a few minutes, Heather would be home and free to cry her stupid little heart out.

"Left at the next street," she said after a moment. Then, "It's the brown house on the right."

Willa pulled into the drive, stopping right behind Penny's truck. Heather sighed. Penny must be over feeding the cats. She guessed she'd have to postpone her cry for a bit.

"Well, thanks for everything," Heather told Willa as she got out of the car. "You want to come in for something to eat or drink?"

Willa just shook her head, nodding toward the car pulling up in front of the house. "Bob's here. We need to get back."

"Okay." Heather got Bonnie and Junior out of the back seat as Willa got out of the driver's side. "I really appreciate it."

"Sure, no problem." She gave Heather the car keys. "Good luck with the Stoneman."

Heather's hand closed around the keys, but she just frowned at the other woman. "With who?"

Willa grinned. "The Stoneman. That's what everyone calls Waterstone because it was suspected he has no heart. Now we aren't so sure.''

''Oh.'' Heather just grasped the handle on Bonnie's carrier with both hands. Alex had a heart, she knew that for certain. He had shown it to her time and time again over the past few weeks, but it wasn't up to her to tell his co-workers that. ''Well, thanks again. If I ever need rescuing from a cabin, I'll call you.''

Willa laughed, then after a wave, hurried down the driveway to the waiting car. Heather watched them drive off, then picked up a box of supplies with one hand and trudged up to her door. Penny was waiting.

''Who was that?'' she asked and took the box from Heather. ''And why are you back so early? I thought you were going away the whole weekend.''

Heather came inside the house, then put the carrier down and opened the door. The kitten raced out, disappearing down the hallway. Junior trotted after her. So much for moral support.

''That was Special Agent Willa Moran,'' she said wearily. ''She drove home with me.''

''Special agent?'' Penny dragged her over to the sofa and pushed her onto it. ''What in the world is going on?''

''I went up to a cabin in the upper peninsula with Alex,'' she said.

''Alex!'' Penny's tone said she was delighted. ''Heather, that's so—''

''I kidnapped him,'' she continued.

''You what?!''

Heather sat up. How had she gotten so tired? ''I thought he had a gambling problem and so I kidnapped him to force-socialize him away from it.''

''You what?'' Penny was laughing so hard Junior

came back out to the living room. "Oh, Heather that's wonderful! And did you succeed?"

"Turns out he didn't need my help," she said and got to her feet. "I'd better unload the car."

"You can't leave it like that," Penny protested. "I want the whole story. You would be so perfect for Alex. You're just—"

"I'm just nothing," Heather said quickly and fought back the tears. "There never was anything between us and now it's over."

She knew that didn't make sense but also knew that any attempt to resay it would only end in tears.

Chapter Thirteen

Alex stopped in the doorway of his darkened living room, sensing someone was there.

"What the hell is with you lately?" Casio snapped. "You haven't been worth a plugged nickel since you came back from the damn cabin. What the hell went on there anyway?"

Alex let his breath out slowly, then walked into the room, leaving the light off. Who had he expected— hoped?—it would be? "Nothing went on," he said.

Oh yeah? Then why couldn't he get Heather out of his mind? Why had he thought of nothing but her this whole week since they had come back? And why had he been hoping against hope that it had been her here waiting for him?

Because he was a damn fool, that was why.

"Where the hell did you go off to this evening?" Casio snapped. "You were supposed to be at Midwest's football game. In case, you're interested they won their home opener big time.''

"That's good.'' Alex took a deep breath, then slowly walked over to the sofa and sat down. "But I got hungry, so I decided to leave and get a bite to eat.''

"You were so hungry, so anxious to eat that you just had to hurry out of the stadium through the team's exit?'' Casio's voice was ripe with anger. "And losing the agents watching your back was just an accident.''

Alex didn't say anything. How could he explain that he'd just had to be alone. That he'd just had to think things through.

"Damn it, Alex. Don't you realize what kind of danger you're in?''

"It comes with the territory,'' Alex snapped.

"You don't have to flirt with it every chance you get.''

Alex looked up. That sounded like something Heather would say. "I don't,'' he argued. "I wasn't. I just wanted to be alone for a while.''

Through the darkness, Alex could vaguely see Casio lean forward. "Look, Alex, we're getting into crunch time here. This isn't the time for you to start mooning over some woman.''

"I'm not,'' Alex snapped and got to his feet. "I just needed some breathing space.''

"You can have plenty of it in a few months. You're due a vacation. Go to the Bahamas. Hawaii. Hell, stay in Chesterton if you want and write poems, but keep your head together now.''

"It is.'' He was fine. He was on the ball. He was as good as ever. He just was beginning to question if it mattered.

Damn, but the house seemed stuffy. He went

through the dining room and threw up the sash on the window in the far wall, leaning his hands on the sill to take deep breaths of the cool night air. Heather's house was all dark, yet even that darkness seemed warm and alive.

"Maybe we shouldn't have put you back here," Casio was saying. "Maybe that was a mistake. But it seemed like a perfect cover."

"It was. It is."

He wondered how Heather was after the trip. He knew she'd gotten home all right because he'd seen her twice since they'd been back. Both times from a distance— him in the house and her going to her car— but she'd looked fine. Well, actually, she'd looked kind of pale but that could have been the light.

"Maybe I'll put in a request for a quicker job for us next time," Casio mused. "Nothing that needs months of deep cover to set up."

"Sure. Sounds good."

He wondered if she told her class all about the deer she saw. Little kids would like that. He frowned out into the night. Why wasn't she surrounded by her own kids? She should be married with a houseful of children. The image both tantalized and tormented. Not married to someone like him, of course, someone that she'd have to worry over, but someone nice and stable and comfortable. Someone she wouldn't have to rescue ever.

"There's a case starting to break in Los Angeles," Casio said. "With a little luck, it could fall just about the time that this one ends and we wouldn't be stuck here in the winter."

"That would be great. Nothing quite like winter here to make you appreciate L.A."

He wasn't still upset about that whole rescue thing. When he'd thought about it—and thought about it he had—he'd had to admit that he'd been overly sensitive. How else was Heather supposed to see him except as someone to rescue? She admitted that he always scared her. That just proved how wrong they were for one another.

Not that he had ever thought they were right for each other. Even if he quit the agency, they still wouldn't be a match. She was so gentle and he was rougher, used to distrust and suspicion.

"One winter here—" Alex stopped and stared out into the night, his eyes piercing the darkness more intensely. He couldn't see anything but his ears picked up the quiet sounds of tires on gravel. A car was in the alley, going slowly. Where were its lights? He ought to see them.

He saw instead the shadowy figure of a man moving in Heather's backyard.

"Damn," Alex said under his breath.

He felt Casio tense, but didn't wait to explain. Before Casio'd had time to stand, Alex was through his kitchen and out the back door, pulling the SIG-Sauer out of his ankle holster as he ran.

Damn it. He should have moved. He should have gotten completely out of this neighborhood. He'd done everything he could think of to keep her out of the cesspool that was his job and she still was in danger. He should never have helped her rescue that kitten. He raced across his driveway and into Heather's yard.

"FBI!" The hell with this undercover crap. "On your knees. Hands above your head."

He was aware of somebody shouting from the direction of the alley, and of Casio rushing by him, but all he really saw was the man in Heather's backyard fall to his knees. Then as he got closer, Alex saw on the ground the knife the man had had in his hand.

Just what had he been planning on using it for? Too many images raced through Alex's mind. Too many terrible images.

"You bastard," Alex cried, and tossed his gun off to the side as he threw himself at the man. "You dirty bastard."

"Please, don't hurt me," the dirtbag screamed as Alex tackled him to the ground.

"I'll teach you to threaten Heather," Alex muttered. He had the man down on the grass and swung an angry fist at him.

"Alex, let up on him," Casio shouted and grabbed ahold of Alex. "Let go of him. We've got him."

Suddenly the floodlights went on in Heather's yard, lighting it up as bright as if it were high noon. Her back door flew open with a crash.

"Everybody freeze," she shouted.

Alex looked up. "Heather?"

She appeared not to have heard him. Or was so scared that she couldn't hear him. Her face was as white as a sheet, but in her hands was a huge old rifle and she was holding it steady.

"The police are on their way," she called out, her voice shaky but loud enough. "So everybody stay nice and still."

What the hell was she doing? "Heather, get back in the house," Alex snapped. "We're taking care of everything out here."

She turned to look at him then and she went paler if that was possible. "Alex?"

"Get back in the house, ma'am," Casio said. "Everything's under control."

But as she turned her gaze to Casio, she raised the gun just a hair and deepened her frown. "Move away from Alex."

Casio muttered something, but stepped back. "There, I'm away from Alex," he said loudly. "But you remember me, ma'am. I work with him. We met up at the cabin."

"For God's sake, Heather," Alex growled as he got to his feet. The scumbag who'd been trying to harm her just lay on the ground, quivering. "Get back in the house before you get hurt."

She lowered her gun slightly as sirens could be heard in the distance. "Are you all right?"

"I'm fine," he snapped and kicked the knife farther from the scumbag. If he could discount the terror running through his veins.

What if he'd come home a half hour later? What if he hadn't been at his window to see the thug in her yard? What if she'd come out to confront him alone?

Anger burned like a flame, licking at his senses, at his emotions until they were all caught up in it. He didn't know who he was angry at—himself mostly, for the danger she'd been in. But her too, for being so gentle and innocent and trusting, and needing his protection even as she denied the need.

"I'm fine," he said again, his voice hoarse with the anger and fear. "I'm always fine. I live for this kind of stuff, remember?"

"Yes. Of course."

Her voice was soft, hollow, filled with pain that tore at him even more. Damn her for being so... so...Heather.

He looked away from her then, picking up his gun as two other agents came into the yard from the alley. With them in handcuffs were the two thugs who had roughed Alex up ten days ago. Casio rushed over to secure the man on the ground as the sirens were coming closer.

He wanted to walk away. He wanted to go meet the local police cars and fill them in on what happened, but somehow he found himself walking slowly over to the steps. He looked up at her.

Heather had lowered the gun into the shadows, but he could still see her pale face. Her eyes were swimming in tears. He wanted nothing more than to go up and take her in his arms, but that wasn't to be. He didn't have the right. He didn't have the courage to face her rejection.

He took a long slow look at her in her teddy bear pajamas and his heart grew even heavier. If he'd ever had any doubts, they were gone now. She was teddy bears and he was handguns.

"Go inside, Heather," he told her softly. Suddenly he was exhausted and it was an effort to speak. "We've got everything under control now. You don't have to worry."

Heather just looked at him and looked down at the gun still in his hand. She nodded, then went silently into her house. She didn't argue, didn't ask him to come in, she just closed her door. He stood for a long moment, staring at it, knowing that inside was warmth and joy and togetherness.

And that it would never be his. No matter what, he didn't belong in her world. He would always be just a rescue to her.

* * *

"Does anyone have any more questions for Officer Tollinger?" Heather asked.

Toto smiled, waiting for inevitable questions about how many bad guys had he caught and did Junior have to wear a badge, but twenty solemn little kids just stared at him from their half circle on the rug. No one spoke, not even any questions about the incident at Heather's house early this morning. They had to know, though. Nothing stayed a secret in this town long.

But Heather just smiled at her class. "Let's thank him for coming then, shall we?"

Twenty separate thank yous sang out in the room.

"Thank you for being such a good audience," he said. "Next time we'll talk about calling 911."

"Miss Mahoney called 911," Barbara Sue Dentman sang out.

Ah, so they did know.

Heather's cheeks turned pink. "We'll talk about that later," she said with a smile and took Toto's arm to lead him to the door.

"Daddy said she should get a medal for—"

"Timmy!" Heather's cheeks went from pink to red. "Officer Tollinger has to get back on duty. We mustn't keep him here with our chatter."

She dragged Toto to the door, obviously associating the comments with him. By the time Junior was out in the hall with them, Toto was laughing openly.

"What's the matter?" he asked, leaning up against the bright red lockers. "Don't you like being a hero to your class?"

"There was nothing heroic about it," she objected, then leaned through the open door to address her class. "Take your traffic signs back to your desks now and put them in your folders. When everyone is sitting up straight and tall, we'll go to recess.''

''Lots of people just ignore noises from outside and wouldn't even get involved enough to call the police.''

''Well, we all know I have no such limits on my involvement. Neighborhood busybody, that's me.''

Toto was surprised by her nervous embarrassed laugh and puzzled by her words. ''Good citizen, I'd say.''

She just sighed and after glancing into the classroom briefly, she leaned against the open door. ''Come on, Toto,'' she said softly. ''You talked to Alex afterward. You know that they had everything under control by the time I went out there to help him. The only good thing was they didn't know my gun was fake.''

Toto just stared at her, feeling as if the air had all been knocked from his lungs. ''You went outside?'' he asked her. Her words only slowly making sense. ''With a gun? With a fake gun?''

She looked startled. ''I thought you'd talked to Alex afterward.''

''I did,'' he snapped. ''But he apparently neglected to mention a few facts. Maybe he knew I'd wring his neck if I found out.''

Little storm clouds appeared in her eyes. ''Why would you wring his neck? He didn't send me out there. It was my choice.''

''It was his fault you were involved at all,'' he pointed out, then bit off his angry words as a class passed behind them. He could feel the kids' curious eyes on him and held his tongue until they went around a corner. ''Damn it, Heather. You could have been hurt.''

''Well, I wasn't. Nothing happened.''

"But something could have." He couldn't believe the chance she had taken. "Damn, a fake gun. Where the hell did you get one?"

She shrugged, looking more embarrassed than anything else. "It goes with your Oz Emerald City guard costume."

"An Oz gun? You went out there with an Oz gun?" Junior whined as if he were as shocked as Toto. Heather glanced around at the long halls. Voices from the classrooms drifted out to them but no one was in sight.

"Would you keep your voices down, you two?" she whispered. "This isn't something I want the whole school to hear about. It's bad enough that I have to live with my stupidity."

"Stupidity?" Yeah, that was one way to look at it. Or else she had been incredibly brave. An uneasy realization began to settle over him. Little timid Heather had done what he'd thought was impossible. "Hell. It looks like I'm gonna have to go to Paris."

"Paris? Why?" Heather repeated, then she must have remembered their bet for she shook her head. "You mean, because of last night? I don't think so. I was supposed to do something brave that had to do with Alex, but I wasn't brave last night. I was scared to death."

He sighed and looked down at Junior, his conscience screaming out in protest. As much as he'd like to weasel out of the bet, he couldn't let her go on with this crazy idea about bravery. He looked up at her and took her hand.

"Heather, that's what bravery is. Being scared to death but doing something anyway. If you weren't scared, it wouldn't be special."

She just frowned at him, wearing her schoolteacher look that said he was talking nonsense. "You don't understand. I almost threw up when I went back inside."

"No, you don't understand. You did something unbelievably brave when you went outside. You can't argue this one away. You did it, and now I have to go to Paris."

"Listen, Miss Bossy Britches, you've had enough olives," Heather said to Victoria. "Go eat your cat food if you're hungry."

The calico cat gave Heather a glare and flounced away, leaving Heather to go back to cutting up the olives for the pasta salad for dinner. It seemed that no one was happy with her these days. Not Victoria, not Toto. Probably not Alex, either, though maybe she was assuming too much. He probably had forgotten she was alive.

If only she could do the same in regard to him, she thought with a sigh.

Aunty Em came into the kitchen. "Table's all set," she said. "Anything else I can do?"

Heather put the olives into the salad and stirred it around. "Just grab the pitcher of iced tea and we're all set." She carried the salad into the dining room. "I'm so glad you called to tell me you were coming into town for a doctor's appointment. What did he say about your knee?"

"That it's fine. Said I could drive. Told him I have been for a couple of weeks." She put the pitcher of iced tea on the table and gave Heather a piercing look. "You've been going on with that investigation of

Alex? I guess you know then that he's talking about leaving."

Heather's heart practically stopped, but she wasn't surprised, was she? He was an undercover agent, for goodness sakes. Once a job was done, of course he would move on. That's what agents did.

Heather put a bright smile on her face to cover the ache in her heart. "Help yourself to everything," she said and picked up the bowl of fruit salad. Her appetite was gone, but she spooned a bit onto her plate anyway. "I'm not surprised to hear that he might be going. I'm just surprised he came back in here the first place."

"Never did trust the man, myself," Aunty Em said.

But Heather had, and look where it had led her. Then she stopped, her hand mid-way to her glass of iced tea. "What is trust anyway?" Heather asked. "And how are we measuring it?"

Aunty Em gave her a sharp look that questioned sanity among other things. "Would you trust him to take care of your cats?" she asked.

Heather looked at Victoria still pouting about having her olives limited and at Henry who was sitting on the edge of the sofa, next to Bonnie as she slept and making sure she didn't fall off. They were so dear to her. Would she trust Alex with them? "Of course," Heather said.

"Would you trust him to manage your money?" Aunty Em pressed on.

Heather nodded and reached for her glass. The tea was cold and refreshing. "Absolutely."

"Would you trust him with your heart?"

Heather froze, then slowly put her glass down. "I don't know. Though if he's leaving, it's a moot point, isn't it?"

"Not if you want him to stay."

"That's not up to me. It's his decision."

Aunty Em sighed long and loudly. "Heather Anne, what world did you grow up in? You never let a man make his own decision. You only let him think he's doing it."

But Heather just shook her head. Aunty Em didn't understand. Not really. "I wouldn't want him to stay if he didn't want to. What good would that be?"

Aunty Em looked as if she were losing patience. "You don't *ask* him to stay, land's sakes. You make him *want* to stay. Good lord, girl, put up a fight. Let him know you're in love with him."

"In love with him?" Heather cried.

Her heart was suddenly frozen with fear. Love was supposed to be soft and warm and dreamy, like riding on a merry-go-round. Being with Alex was like riding a roller coaster, with sudden drops and wild highs and all the while a tension that took her breath away.

"I'm fond of him," she said. "But I'm not in love with him."

"Of course you are," Aunty Em snapped. "I can see it in your eyes every time I mention the bum's name and you've had that dreamy look in your eyes since you came back from your Labor Day vacation."

"No." Heather was definite. "I can't be in love with Alex. He doesn't love me back."

The older woman frowned. "A man like that is too afraid to admit to himself he's in love. If you want him, you're going to have to rescue him from his fears." She reached for her iced tea, then growled at it. "Helping to keep that bum here. I don't believe it. I need a beer."

* * *

"Looks like you're going to have another commendation in your file," Casio said, hands folded on the desk. His smile actually touched his eyes.

But it didn't touch Alex. "What the hell for?" he asked.

"For the great job you did on this case." Casio smirked. "Sure as hell not for your sweet personality."

Alex wasn't into jokes and innuendos. He was exhausted and could barely handle straight, clear conversation. "You want to clue me in? Or are you going to just play games all evening?"

"Sorry, I just can't believe it." Casio leaned back in his chair, putting his hands behind his head. "The case is broken. That guy you decked in your neighbor's yard is singing his head off. And since he was one of the operation's bookkeepers, he's got a lot of interesting verses to his song."

That didn't make sense. "A bookkeeper? What was a bookkeeper doing there?"

Casio shook his head. "Trying to earn approval apparently. The other guys all had records and he thought they didn't respect him."

Alex frowned at his supervisor. "So he figured attacking Heather was going to make him a big shot?"

"I'm not sure what he had planned. I'm not sure he knew. He just thought by scaring her, they'd have more control over you. Now he's singing so fast, we can barely keep up."

Alex leaned back in his chair. "So the job's over," he said.

That meant Heather would be safe. It also meant he'd really be moving on, not just moving away from Chesterton to keep her safe while he finished this job.

He'd get another assignment and move to another location.

He frowned; the idea made him even more tired.

"The job's over and we're all stars," Casio was saying. "Commendations for all of us."

"Great." Like it mattered anymore how many commendations were in his file. "So what's next on the agenda?"

Casio shrugged. "Who knows? This thing went down so fast, they haven't even begun to think of where to send us next. I guess that means a nice vacation is in order."

Vacation? Going to yet another place alone? Hadn't that been the story of his life? He stood and wandered over to the window, looking down on the backsides of some nondescript brick buildings. Nondescript. Anonymous. Could be in any town, any country even.

Just like him. Not a part of anything.

Alex turned. "What about my teaching job? Won't this leave them in the lurch? They were awfully cooperative when we were setting this up."

Casio shook his head. "Keep it if you want. You could probably finish out the fall semester."

Did he want to? The idea was appealing, but was it wise? He couldn't go on living next to Heather. The past week had been pure hell for him. Seeing her and not being a part of her life anymore. It was like slow, excruciating torture.

But the nights were the absolute worst. That's when she slipped into his bed, close enough for him to feel the heat of her body but not close enough to wrap his arms around. She spent the whole night dancing out on the edge of his conscious so that he woke up exhausted in the morning.

"I wouldn't mind finishing out the semester," Alex said as he came back toward the desk. "But maybe I'll sublet a place near campus. No reason to make that long commute anymore."

Casio just looked at him. "Sure. Whatever you want. Just stay in touch."

Alex nodded, then left. *Whatever he wanted.* But what did he want?

Moving in a daze through the rapidly deepening shadows of dusk, he got in his car and started on home, not really aware of his surroundings until he was well down the Dan Ryan Expressway. An exit sign plucked at his memory and, without thinking, he pulled off the expressway. Bright streetlights drew him down the depressing streets until he came to the shady gambling den. It was empty now, shut down by the feds once the bookkeeper had started to sing.

Alex pulled up to the curb, looking across at the empty parking lot and the sagging decrepit building next to it. The streetlights threw long shadows across the landscape, making it all look lonelier and more empty.

But then in his mind's eye, he saw something else. A blond, blue-eyed little elf coming to his rescue, taking his heart into the shelter of her arms and, most cruelly of all, giving him a taste of what life could be like.

He turned off the motor and got out of his car, walking over to the far side of the gravel lot. The area where Heather had rescued him. Maybe he was hoping he could capture the essence of her and lock the memory away where it would never touch him again. Fat chance.

He leaned on the chain-link fence, staring out at the

dirty streets and the dilapidated houses, looking even more depressing in the faint light of the night. He should be glad the assignment was over so fast and so safely. Bad guys locked up. Nobody hurt. Well, not in ways that showed.

So why was he feeling so down?

Maybe the undercover work had lost its edge. Maybe he ought to look at teaching for real. See if Midwest would keep him on or send out some inquiries to other area schools. Hell, why local? It wasn't like he had a reason to stay around. Heather wasn't going to forgive him for his deception.

Shaking his head, he turned to go but a sound made him stop. He turned to see the brown-and-white cat staring at him. It looked even skinnier than before.

"So, you got any advice for me?" Alex asked.

The cat just sat there and stared at him.

"Yeah, right. What decision is there to make?" Alex said with a sigh. "It isn't like I haven't burned all my bridges but one. I'm sitting here dreaming, but that's all it is. A dream. I lied to her. I scared her. I tried to keep her safe and all I did was end up hurting her."

The cat came a few steps closer. It's steps were wobbly, Alex noticed. And now that he looked closer, everything about the animal seemed weary and weak.

"I bet you need a meal, don't you?" he said and looked around. A hot dog vendor was down the street. "I'll be right back," he told the cat.

He half expected the cat to be gone when he got back, but the animal was still there. Alex broke the hot dog into small pieces and tossed them over the chain-link fence. His aim was pretty good, but the animal just barely sniffed at them, then turned away.

"Wrong kind?" he asked and frowned. "Good thing Heather isn't here. She'd try to catch you and take you home."

The cat just looked up at that, blinking his green eyes, but Alex wasn't fooled. This cat had been living on the streets too long; it was too far gone to be rescued.

He swallowed the lump that suddenly appeared in his throat. "Guess we have a lot in common," he said. "We're both beyond help."

Still the cat stared and finally Alex just turned to leave. He expected the cat would go also, but when he turned back a few steps later, the cat was still there. Still staring.

"What? You think you could change?" he asked it. "Well, you're fooling yourself. Sure, a nice warm home sounds great. Someone there to call your own. But what if you really hurt her already? It's not even fair to ask her to forgive me."

But then he looked at the awful streets and the cat's thin body and sighed. The night suddenly seemed full of dangers. Alex sighed. Just because he was beyond hope, it didn't mean that this little fellow was, too.

"Okay, maybe she'd take you in. You didn't lie to her."

He pulled a battered cardboard box from a nearby trash bin, telling himself he was crazy. The cat would run when Alex tried to get close. And if it didn't, it would never agree to get in a box. And even if it did, Heather would probably slam the door in his face.

Well, he knew that last one was wrong. Heather might slam the door on him, but she'd take the cat first.

When he went back to the fence, the cat was still

there. It stayed even when Alex vaulted over the fence into the weed-and-gravel-strewn lot.

"Okay, this is the plan," Alex told him. "You get in the box and we go to Heather's house. If you're smart, you'll pretend you don't know me."

Chapter Fourteen

Was she in love with Alex or not? Heather spent the evening fretting over the question as she finished Toto's costume, but coming to no real answer.

When her mother called around nine, Heather was thoroughly relieved. A distraction from her torturous thoughts.

"Are you all right?" her mother asked, worry pouring through the telephone line.

"Of course, I am," Heather said. She settled comfortably into the corner of the sofa. Henry came over and snuggled with her. "Why wouldn't I be?"

"I was just talking to Emma Donnelly and she told me you'd been stranded in the woods of upper Michigan over the Labor Day weekend."

Heather just closed her eyes and laid against the sofa back. Good old Aunty Em. What else had she told? "Mom, I wasn't stranded." Heather said gently. "I went up there to stay in a summer cabin Dorothy told me about for a few days."

"A summer cabin? Oh, that sounds lovely." Her mother sounded visibly relieved. "You don't know what I was picturing when she told me."

Whatever her mother was picturing now was probably far from reality, but Heather wasn't going to argue. "Well, you needn't have worried. It was very nice. And very relaxing to get away from everything."

"That's so good to hear. What did you do up there? Visit antique shops and eat in tea rooms?"

Heather hesitated, her comfy, cozy feeling slipping away slightly. She wasn't going to lie, but she hated to get her mother upset. "Not exactly," she said carefully. "The cabin wasn't in town."

"Not in town?" The worry was back. "Where was it then? Not—" a horrified pause "—in the woods?"

Heather sighed and realized Henry was frowning at her. Her agitation must have disturbed her petting. She made a conscious effort to relax. The woods had been the least of the dangers, as it turned out. "Mom, it was lovely there. I saw a family of deer and all kinds of birds and turtles."

"Deer and turtles! My heavens, Heather," her mother cried. "What were you thinking of? They could have been rabid!"

"I suppose."

"Don't you remember that little girl Great Aunt Millie's cousin knew? The one that got bit by a rabid weasel and swelled up and died a horrible death?"

"Of course, I remember." It had been the food for years of nightmares. "But I was safe. Really. I didn't get bit by anything." Her nagging draggy sleeplessness came from her troubles with Alex, not any animal or insect bite.

"Tell me you didn't leave your window open at night," her mother added, the panic in her voice growing. "And risk catching pneumonia and dying from a terrible high fever like the little boy that used to live next door to old Mrs. Schubert's mother's best friend."

"Mom, I'm fine." The window had been open, but she hadn't caught anything. Not a chill. Not Alex's heart.

"Oh, heavens. Next you'll be telling me you went out in a storm and didn't even think about the dangers from lightning."

She had, hadn't she? Though the bolt of lightning that had hit her hadn't been from the storm, but from Alex's touch.

"Mom, you can't live your whole life being afraid."

"Heather, this doesn't sound like you at all. What's come over you?"

"Nothing, it's just…"

It was just what? What had happened to her up there in the woods? Maybe she had been bit—by a love bug. And caught a love fever, and maybe that bolt of lightning had really been Cupid's arrow.

"Toto told me I was brave the other day," she said slowly. "I think maybe he was right."

"Gracious." Her mother gasped. "What did you do?"

The actual events were no longer important, but the rush of sudden belief in herself was. "I think I fell in love."

"You what! With who?"

Heather heard a noise from outside—a car pulling into Alex's driveway—and jumped to her feet. It was now or never. She had to fight for him while she had the chance. "Mom, I have to go. I think Alex is home."

"Alex?" her mother shrieked. "Not Alex Waterstone?"

"Yes, Mom. Alex Waterstone. And this is going to be a major rescue. Wish me luck."

Alex pulled the box from the front seat of his car, looking inside the half-open top. The cat looked back at him. "Heather'll take good care of you," Alex said. "And you'll like her. She's—"

Across the driveway, her door opened and she came racing out in her teddy bear pajamas. His heart wanted to weep at the sight of her, but he forced back the feelings. He was moving—just this sight of her was enough to convince him it was the only way to retain his sanity—but right now, her sudden appearance alarmed him.

"What's wrong?" he asked as she came around to his side of the car. Even with her face in the shadows, he could sense her urgency.

"Nothing's wrong," she told him. "We need to talk. Aunty Em said you're leaving."

He sighed slightly. "The job's over. That guy I caught in your backyard the other night is giving us lots of information. Enough for dozens of indictments."

"So you won't be getting beat up anymore?"

He didn't know how to answer that. "I can pretty much guarantee you won't find me unconscious on your lawn again."

But she wasn't fooled by his wordplay. "Alex Waterstone, when are you going to stop racing across the seawall?''

''This is different,'' he said. ''This is my job.''

''So why can't you stay here and still do your job?''

''I don't have that type of job. You know that.''

She came a step closer so that her essence threatened to overwhelm him if he didn't stay strong. ''Would it make a difference if I told you I didn't want you to go?'' she said softly.

The pleading in her voice merged with the want in his heart and tore at him. ''Heather, don't. I'm not the type to settle down in one place.''

He looked down at the box in his arms. Best get on with it and go. Maybe he would leave tonight. Go to a hotel until he thought out what to do. ''Anyway, I brought you something.''

She looked at the box, then up at him. ''That's for me?''

He carried the box over to a patch of light from her back door and put it on the ground. ''It's a cat,'' he said and lifted the lid slightly. ''He was living—''

But even as he spoke, the cat pushed aside the flimsy cover and leapt out of the box. For a half second, he stood there on the driveway, looking at the two of them, his white-spotted nose atwitch. Then he turned and darted into Heather's backyard.

''Damn,'' Alex muttered and shoved the box to one side as he hurried after the cat. ''He got in the box without a fuss and rode the whole way in the car without a murmur. Why'd he run now?''

Heather stopped at the edge of the yard and looked around. ''Where'd you find him?''

''By the gambling den. He's been living on the

streets there and…'' It sounded so weak. ''I just couldn't leave him there.''

Heather turned to look at him, her eyes narrowing in the light coming in from the alley. ''What's his name?'' she asked.

Name? Did he have to have a name for Heather to like him? ''Winston,'' Alex said.

''Oh, really?'' She smiled as if she knew some secret and then walked slowly into the yard. ''Winston,'' she called out softly. ''Come on, sweetie pie. Come on out, Winston.''

It was lighter back here. A mixed blessing. It meant that Alex could see Heather better, see her soft and gentle manners, her radiant beauty, and her womanly curves that set his heart afire just watching her. But at the same time, it hurt to see her and know that this might be the last time.

She stooped down and looked under a bush. ''Hi, there little fellow. Did you get scared?''

Alex walked slowly over. He'd help her catch the cat and then he'd go. And while he was here, he would remain unmoved, untouched by her nearness.

''He in there?'' Alex asked as he bent down next to her. A whiff of some flowery scent stirred his senses and he had to fight off a growing awareness of her.

''Yep. Just a little ways back.'' Heather sat down on the ground.

Alex knelt next to her, not too close, but not too far away, either. Then the cat moved and Alex had to slide a little closer to her to keep him in sight.

''He doesn't look too scared,'' Alex noted.

''No, he doesn't,'' Heather agreed. ''But that doesn't mean anything. Sometimes the ones most scared of love act the bravest. You just have to be more patient with them.''

''How can you tell who needs the extra patience?''

Heather turned to look at him. ''They're the ones who run from love.''

The conversation had suddenly turned and he felt a tightness in his chest. An ache in the region of his heart that he knew was all emotions.

''Heather, it just wouldn't work. I'm all wrong for you.''

''You know, I never expected you to be so afraid,'' she said.

But he wasn't going to be drawn into that argument. ''Damn right I'm afraid,'' he said. ''I'm scared to death that I'd hurt you. You deserve better than me.''

''It's not a matter of deserving,'' she said. ''It's who your heart picks.''

''Well, tell your heart to pick again. And better.''

''What does your heart say?''

''I don't know. I haven't asked it.''

''Maybe you should.''

He moved away, as if reason would penetrate if he wasn't so close to her. ''Heather. I'm like that cat over there. I lived on the street too long to be tamed.''

''No, you're both just afraid of trusting.'' She came closer, taking his hand in hers and holding it tightly. ''I don't think you're afraid you'll hurt me at all. I think you're afraid I'll hurt you.''

''That's crazy.'' He tried to pull his hand away but she wouldn't let go. ''I know you wouldn't hurt me. You're the gentlest person I know.''

''Your father was a good person, but he hurt you,'' she pointed out. ''And I think fear of being hurt like that has kept you from getting too close to anyone else again.''

He wanted to argue with her. He wanted to tell her that she was wrong, but he had this awful feeling that she wasn't.

''And I can't promise that I won't,'' she said softly. ''Who knows what the future holds? But I'd rather have a wonderful today and a sad tomorrow than a lifetime of ordinary.''

He looked at her. A small ray of her warmth was starting to melt some block of stubbornness in his heart. He wanted her so badly. Not just in the sexual sense, but in every way. She made him so complete.

''Are you sure you want to take me on?'' he asked. ''I love you more than life itself, but I'm a moody, brooding sort who may always be afraid of real emotions.''

''And don't forget your tendency to race across seawalls,'' she added.

He pulled her into his arms at that. ''Hey, I haven't done that for years.''

He kissed her then, a raging, powerful ravishing of her lips. The force of the past week of misery came exploding from him. He needed her so much, needed to feel her next to him, needed to feel her beside him. Needed to know that she was always there for him.

His hands crushed her to him, his mouth drew his very life from her. She fit up against him so perfectly, in his arms just right. His mouth pulled at hers, his hands roamed over her back, his arms tightened around her. He couldn't let her go, not ever.

But then the driving hunger changed and his lips gentled on hers. She was his life, his heart, his soul. She gave his existence meaning and focus and courage.

He was suddenly ready to brave all sorts of dangers. All he needed was his hand in hers.

He let go of her slightly and smiled into those wonderful blue eyes. Everything seemed ready to fall into place. "How would you feel about having a college professor for a husband?"

"You're quitting the agency?" Her hand gently touched his cheek. "You don't have to, you know. I'll be here for you whenever, whatever."

But his shook his head. "Nope. I'm through with that. I've found that love is the scariest risk of all. I don't need any other thrills."

She smiled and melted back into his arms just as they heard a small sound to one side. Still in each other's arms, they looked down. The brown-and-white cat had come out of the bushes and was sitting next to them.

Heather just laughed and reached one hand down slowly to pet him. "Hi, Winston. Welcome to the family."

Epilogue

"I now pronounce you man and wife," the minister said as he closed his book. "You may kiss the bride."

"Will I ever!" Alex muttered with a devilish grin as he scooped Heather up into his arms. "Mrs. Waterstone, prepare to be kissed."

Heather just laughed and threw her arms around his neck, pulling him close to her. Their lips met in a wild joyous celebration of love. Sweeter than cotton candy. More spectacular than fireworks. More lasting than love itself.

The minister coughed discreetly and they pulled apart with smiles only for each other. Tucking her hand in Alex's, they hurried from the chapel into the bright Nevada sunlight. Once outside though, their steps slowed as if time were standing still.

Heather stared down at her small bouquet of white

roses and the simple white dress she'd bought before they'd left Chesterton this morning. Nothing extravagant, but she'd never felt so beautiful, never felt so loved. She tucked her arm in his and they walked slowly over to the small garden in back.

"Are you sure this was okay?" Heather asked. "You're sure you didn't want more time to think it over?"

He just smiled down at her, his eyes so filled with love that she almost cried.

"More time for what?" he asked as he took her once more in his arms. "I haven't slept since I asked you to marry me, afraid you were going to come to your senses and change your mind. I was only too happy to fly out here and get married."

"We could have waited until after the Oz Festival."

"And have some slick-talking Oz groupie sweep you off your feet?" His arms tightened possessively around her. "Not a chance, lady. I wanted my ring on your finger without delay. I was ready to fly here the other night as soon as we got Winston into your quarantine room."

"I had school the next day."

"So I waited patiently for the weekend." He kissed her lightly on the forehead, then more slowly on the cheek. "Now, I've done all the waiting I can."

She touched his cheek, almost unable to believe that he was hers now. Her ring glittered in the sunlight and the scent of her bouquet seemed to envelope them. The knowledge that she was so loved made her feel strong, made her feel brave. Made her feel adventurous.

"You poor thing," she teased. "I imagine you can

hardly wait to get to bed. The last three nights without sleep. You must be exhausted.''

His arms swung her into the air as his laughter danced around them. ''Not hardly, my love,'' he said. ''My precious, precious love.''

* * * * *

Don't miss book three in Andrea Edwards'
delightful miniseries THE BRIDAL CIRCLE
when Karin finds true love in
PREGNANT & PRACTICALLY MARRIED,
available November 1999, only from
Silhouette Special Edition.

*This August 1999, the legend
continues in Jacobsville*

DIANA PALMER

LOVE WITH A
LONG, TALL TEXAN

A trio of brand-new short stories featuring
three irresistible Long, Tall Texans

GUY FENTON, LUKE CRAIG
and CHRISTOPHER DEVERELL...

This August 1999, Silhouette brings readers an
extra-special collection for Diana Palmer's legions
of fans. Diana spins three unforgettable stories of
love—Texas-style! Featuring the men you can't get
enough of from the wonderful town of Jacobsville,
this collection is a treasure for all fans!

*They grow 'em tall in the saddle in Jacobsville—and
they're the best-looking, sweetest-talking men to be
found in the entire Lone Star state. They are proud,
hardworking men of steel and it will take
the perfect woman to melt their hearts!*

**Don't miss this collection of original
Long, Tall Texans stories...available in
August 1999 at your favorite retail outlet.**

FOR THE CHILDREN

Sometimes families are made in the most unexpected ways!

Don't miss this heartwarming new series from
Silhouette Special Edition®, Silhouette Romance®
and popular author

DIANA WHITNEY

Every time matchmaking lawyer
Clementine Allister St. Ives brings a couple
together, it's for the children...
and sure to bring romance!

August 1999
I NOW PRONOUNCE YOU MOM & DAD
Silhouette Special Edition #1261
Ex-lovers Powell Greer and Lydia Farnsworth knew *nothing*
about babies, but Clementine said they needed to learn—fast!

September 1999
A DAD OF HIS OWN
Silhouette Romance #1392
When Clementine helped little Bobby find his father, Nick Purcell
appeared on the doorstep. Trouble was, Nick wasn't Bobby's dad!

October 1999
THE FATHERHOOD FACTOR
Silhouette Special Edition #1276
Deirdre O'Connor's temporary assignment from Clementine
involved her handsome new neighbor, Ethan Devlin—and
adorable twin toddlers!

Available at your favorite retail outlet.

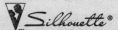

Silhouette ® SPECIAL EDITION ®
LINDSAY McKENNA
delivers two more exciting books in her heart-stopping new series:

MORGAN'S MERCENARIES III — THE HUNTERS

Coming in July 1999:
HUNTER'S WOMAN
Special Edition #1255
Ty Hunter wanted his woman back from the moment he set his piercing gaze on her. For despite the protest on Dr. Catt Alborak's soft lips, Ty was on a mission to give the stubborn beauty everything he'd foolishly denied her once—his heart, his soul—and most of all, his child....

And coming in October 1999:
HUNTER'S PRIDE
Special Edition #1274
Devlin Hunter had a way with the ladies, but when it came to his job as a mercenary, the brooding bachelor worked alone. Until his latest assignment paired him up with Kulani Dawson, a feisty beauty whose tender vulnerabilities brought out his every protective instinct—and chipped away at his proud vow to never fall in love....

Look for the exciting series finale in early 2000—when MORGAN'S MERCENARIES: THE HUNTERS comes to Silhouette Desire®!

Available at your favorite retail outlet.

Silhouette ®